Praise for *The Village Sang to the Sea*

"*The Village Sang to the Sea* is a uniquely haunting book, unlike any novel - fantasy or mainstream - I've read in a long time. By turns touching, funny, and truly frightening, it goes its own deliberate, constantly surprising way to an immensely satisfying climax. I've no idea whether or not a critic might call it 'magical realism,' but under any official designation, it's quite simply a beauty--in the fullest meaning of the word."

- Peter S. Beagle, World Fantasy Lifetime Achievement Award winner and author of *The Last Unicorn*

"*The Village Sang to the Sea* is that rarity: a book that delicately and perfectly captures the magic we all know underlies the world, the sure knowledge that things mean more than they appear. Brad is a real American boy in a real Italian village, but he can see clearly what the rest of us must infer. In prose both precise and lyrical, Bruce McAllister captures Brad's vision and shares it richly. You will not forget this book. Not ever."

- Nancy Kress, Hugo and Nebula awards winner and author of *Beggars in Spain*

"*The Village Sang to the Sea*, like any profound work of art, works on more than one level; that is, it is more than it seems to be. It works in profound, dark counterpoint, the story concealed, then revealed like the six-part conclusion of Bruckner's Eighth Symphony. Sharp and lingering...."

- Barry Malzberg, John W. Campbell Memorial Award winner r of *Beyond Apollo*

D0839108

THE VILLAGE SANG
TO THE SEA

A Memoir of Magic

BRUCE MCALLISTER

AEON PRESS BOOKS

First published by Aeon Press 2013
All stories © 2013 Bruce McAllister

ISBN: 978-0-9534784-9-1

Cover image: permission to reprint *The Castle of Lerici in the Gulf of La Spezia* by James Hakewill (© 2013) is kindly granted by the Indianapolis Museum of Art.

Cover design by Ben McAllister and John Kenny

Text design and typesetting by John Kenny
Printed and bound by Lightning Source

Typesetting Fonts: Book Antiqua and Perpetua Titling MT

For information on this and other books published by Aeon Press, visit www.albedo1.com

To brother Jack, who knows
and Barry, midwife yet again

Acknowledgements

'Prologue' (under the title 'Seventh Daughter') was originally published in *The Magazine of Fantasy and Science Fiction* and reprinted in *The Year's Best Fantasy 5* (Hartwell/Cramer).

'Poison', in a different version, was originally published in *Asimov's Science Fiction* and reprinted in *The Year's Best Fantasy 8* (Hartwell/Cramer).

'Ombra', in a different version, was originally published in *Glimmer Train*.

'The Bleeding Child' was originally published in *Cemetery Dance*.

'Mary' (first and second part) was originally published in *Lady Churchill's Rosebud Wristlet*.

'The Woman Who Waited Forever' was originally published in *Asimov's Science Fiction*.

'Heart of Hearts' was originally published in *Albedo One*.

'Epilogue' (under the title 'Sun and Stone'), in a different version, was originally published in *Image: A Journal of Art, Faith and Mystery*.

Table of Contents

I

PROLOGUE

The Seventh Daughter
by
Brad Lattimer
from *The Village and Other Stories*
New Millennium Books, 2012

The American boy lived with his parents in a small villa high on a hillside above a cove where young people danced at night, laughing and shouting, their voices rising through the olive trees to him as he fell asleep. Sometimes he did not know which was the real story: The Ligurian Sea below him in the night, where a poet had drowned long ago; the laughter and shouting below him that drowned out the whispers of that sea and the mutterings of that poet; the boyish face he saw in the mirror when he dared to look; the seashells he collected, whose Latin names he memorized; the things he made of clay and words that only he knew about. It didn't matter, he told himself--it was all real and yet it was not--but the question was always there as he fell asleep and woke.

In the bottom drawer of his bedroom dresser, with every color of modeling clay, he had made a world and knew its story perfectly. "The Seven Daughters of Satan," he called it. He built very carefully the valley, the forest and the seven villages where the daughters of Satan, who had abandoned them, grew up. The men of the villages were scared of the daughters, beautiful as they were, because they knew who they were. The daughters showed no dark gifts, no witch's skills or demonic tendencies, but the men of the villages felt it: The waiting. The waiting for him. The entire valley and the mountains that surrounded it were waiting. If you held your breath and stayed entirely still, you could even hear it: The ticking of God's great clock. The hour didn't matter. What mattered was that the ticking never stopped. The men heard it as they stared, hearts breaking, at the faces of the seven daughters, and did not take a step toward them. The daughters did not understand.

They could not hear the ticking. They did not know why the men stared.

The daughters kept more and more to themselves and the men said less and less. A child might run up to one of the girls and say something, hand something to her, take something away, even play with her. But the adults never took such a chance. The daughters grew more sullen, their white faces and their red lips once like seven Sleeping Beauties, but now like fading ghosts. *He will return,* the villagers whispered to themselves, and they maintained their distance.

Inside the daughters' thatched house, inside its tiny doorways--where they had grown up, sleeping side by side on mats on a clay floor--they had a deaf nanny to watch over them. The nanny could not hear the ticking either, and was growing blinder each year as well.

Each daughter had a dresser built years ago, when they were little, by men from the villages. In each daughter's dresser, which had been painted the color of blood, there were seven drawers, and in the top drawer, made of clay and fashioned by the nanny's son (who lived with them but slept in a separate room) was a replica of the village in which the daughter had been conceived and born. The villagers knew that late at night little people of clay, homunculi, were brought to life by supernatural power and moved through the clay village in each drawer to entertain the lonely daughter it belonged to.

One day the boy, who was not from this valley but knew its story, found the smallest and prettiest of the daughters and stood before her, big and gangly in his dark suit, his skin on fire from self-consciousness. She was, he saw, as scared as he was.

"Are you my father?" she asked.

"No," he answered. "I am a boy."

She nodded, smiled a pale smile, and let him take her in his arms, dancing her across the cobbles of the village square to music that came not from guitars or other instruments, but from the throats of the villagers as they stood and watched and began to hum, the sound soon filling the valley like the voice of God.

Before long every daughter was dancing, and the clock stopped its ticking.

When strains of 1950's songs like "Diana" and "Heavenly Shades of Night" and "The Great Pretender" and all the others reached the boy from the lido, that outdoor dance floor in the cove far below his bedroom window, he would lie in bed thinking of the boys and girls--a few years older than he and flirting in another language--dancing. He would not get up. He would not turn on a light. He would listen to the songs until he fell asleep. As he slept he dreamed long, adventurous dreams of strange places, heroes and creatures worthy of legends, but also shorter dreams about hills covered with vipers and funerals of his relatives and a little boat in a storm, sinking, and it was these shorter dreams that came true. Why they did, he didn't know. It made no sense, but what did in life anyway? The longer dreams became stories which he wrote in longhand and kept secret from his parents in the drawer right below the seven daughters, which he also kept secret. The ones that came true he never wrote down. It frightened him to do so. When he woke from his dreams, he would go to school with his friends from the village, or go down to the wharf by himself to find seashells among the colorful fish in the nets, or walk along the dirt road that led from his house past the ancient walls and their lizards to the Hotel Byron. One day his parents said it: "That hotel is too new. It couldn't be where they lived." "Who?" the boy asked. "Mary Shelley and her husband Percy," they answered. "The woman who wrote that book. The one about the monster. Frankenstein." Not long after he would learn from someone that Percy, her husband, the poet, had drowned one stormy night in his little boat as he made his way from Viareggio up the coast back to this very village.

When the boy was back in his own country and the dreams--the ones that came true--had stopped, and he no longer made things of clay to put in drawers and lizards no longer watched him from the walls, he learned that that woman, Mary, had dreamed her dream--the one that had become her sad and terrible book--in that little fishing village, too.

Often, years later, when he was a man and had a wife and children, he would try to remember what had happened to the drawer and its mountains, valley, villages and people of clay. "The Seven Daughters of Satan," he had called it. This he could remember, but he could not remember what had happened to that clay. Did it matter? Weren't people--your wife, your children--what mattered? Then one night, as he lay beside his wife, she put her arm over him and whispered in the dark, "Thank you for setting us free," and he knew which story it was and how there would never be anything as real (because love is what makes things real) as this.

II

MAGIC

Some places have more magic than they should. For our own good, I mean. That's the only way I know to say it, and ever will. Sometimes it's a magic that shows you God's face. Sometimes it's a magic that shows you the rotten teeth of witches and would just as soon kill you as look at you. Sometimes it's a magic whose plans for you you'll never understand — a magic that plays with you, teases you, haunts you for months or years, tries to change you into something you're not, and you don't know whether you're supposed to laugh or cry or run or just stand there and let it have its way. A magic that makes you write stories when you're young, feeling it for the first time, and keep writing them until the day you die --because it has stories it wants you to tell.

The little fishing village on the Ligurian coast of Northern Italy was like that; but when you're twelve or thirteen, you don't know any different. You think life is supposed to have magic. You think there are supposed to be forces you don't understand, and grown-ups who can wield them. At that age you barely know what's real or not — especially when you're the kind of dreamy, bookish, animal-loving kid I was — and you take what life throws at you: Your mother crying over your baby brother, who died when he was one, cannot stop crying, and gets angry so she won't be sad; the man without a throat down by the wharf, a red handkerchief covering the hole, his handkerchief slipping as he talks to you, which he does by spitting air, by making words that way; your teacher, a hunchback who, with a lisp that softens everything he says, teaches you and the other boys in the little gray classroom with its single light bulb and heater that never works, and loves a woman in the next village, but will never be able to marry; and the uppity green lizards on the ancient stone wall by your house, staring at you way too long, blinking, doing their little pushups to tell you whose wall

13

it is; and when you look at them you're sure you hear a voice chattering in your head, saying, "We're so pretty, Brad. Don't you think so? Don't you wish you were as pretty as we are, and as brave? Don't you wish you had scales instead of skin just like us?"

Or the three witches that live in stone huts in the olive groves and poison cats. Or the tiny village of Magusa up the hill, its red doorways barely big enough to let men through, where things that should not walk the groves in moonlight do walk them, and a baby cries in the night forever.

Or the old German hospital two coves down the coastal road that isn't as empty as people think it is. Or the strange girl who makes designs on the sand with seashells and can make those seashells dance in the air if she likes you, if she has chosen you to be the *one* — the one who will die with her.

Or the great stag and the quiet owl in the sacred forest your parents take you to when you fall ill--praying for you, though they never pray.

Or the rash you get from the sea — the one that will not go away, that wants to change you forever.

And why wouldn't this village — charming Lerici by the sea --have magic? It is the village where, according to local legend, the writer Mary Shelley dreamed the dream that became her story about a monster who, brought to life by a scientist, only wanted love; and the same village where, whether she dreamed her dream there or not, her husband, the great Romantic poet Percy Bysshe Shelley did drown returning in his boat one night from the carnival city of Viarreggio, having seen portents of his own death for weeks before.

If it had magic for them--as it apparently also did for Neolithic people six thousand years ago who used the hole in the great stone cliff near the village to view the constellation Cassiopeia at the right time of the year--why wouldn't it for a boy, one who didn't yet know how like death magic can be?

When my father was told that the Navy needed him in the Italian port city of La Spezia, to help run an anti-submarine warfare center during the Cold War, he had answered, "No, thank you." He was happy—we were all happy—in the pretty Navy town of San Diego, California, where we lived on a base with spacious quarters, a beach, access to boats of many sizes, tennis courts, even a barbershop and little store; and where my mother could be the Navy wife she'd always wanted to be. But you don't say "No" to the Navy; and, like the gods calling to the heroes of old, they asked him again, and he knew he had to say "Yes."

We would live not in the industrial port itself, my mother announced one day, but in one of the little fishing villages to the south of La Spezia, because they were pretty and what a shame it would be to live in a very gray city we could find anywhere. It was a story she was telling, my father and I knew--a story about the sadness of anything gray, about the happiness of beauty and hope. It was a story about my brother, who'd died of encephalitis as a baby when I was five; and about a village that might make her forget. If we lived in a little fishing village, she was saying, she would not be sad; she could be happy, as she had been in San Diego. We wanted, my father and I, to see her happy; and we also liked the idea of a fishing village ourselves. How wonderful. How *magical*.

It was a beautiful village she chose, and for that I am grateful. My father, always generous, paid for a tutor that first summer so that I would be able to attend the local school, if it would have me. "No sitting listening to English and eating cheeseburgers at Livorno," my mother, who was a teacher and loved the world when she wasn't sad, said to anyone who would listen. She was right. Why live in a place as beautiful as the region of Liguria if you were going to sit in an English-language school on an American Navy base for six hours? And spend two hours on a bus coming and going.

Those who ran Lerici's one school, kind people that they were, said, "Of course he can attend! We need a boy with a very round face and freckles who speaks broken Italian and has orange hair. We have never had one before." If they didn't say this, they certainly thought it. I would be their "American boy," and they would treat me the way only a village that had survived the Romans, the Dark and Middle Ages, the great city-states of Europe, and countless wars could.

The school building was old, the boys and girls segregated, the face of King Emmanuel defaced on its outer wall by the Fascists of a war now fifteen years passed, and the face of Mussolini, positioned to replace the King's face, defaced soon after that by someone just as unhappy with Fascism as with royalty. Because I was of the upper class—the families of military officers always were--I would attend the *scuola media*, the academic track that led to the *ginnasio* and the *liceo* of the educated. The technical school was for the sons and daughters of laborers, of Communists who nevertheless attended church devoutly, of those who lived in the old part of town or worked the olive groves or took the bus to La Spezia for their union jobs.

A fourteenth century castle--one fought over centuries before by the forces of Pisa and Genoa, not to mention the jealous Archbishops of Pisa and the powerful Malaspina family--looked down on Lerici's cove and wharf, where every morning the bright fishing boats left early and returned at midday with their catches for the stands on the wharf and the fishwives who kept there all afternoon. A jetty of great, jagged rocks brought from Piombino, near Napoleon's Elba, protected the little boats in the cove from the very kind of storm that had drowned that famous poet over a century before.

If you had reason to take the coastal road north to La Spezia, you would wind first through the cove where Mary and Percy --and their good friend Lord Byron--had lived in a big, dark villa that was no longer there; past another cove where a German army hospital sat abandoned up a road; then through the tiny village of San Terenzo, and its cove, where the woman loved by our hunchback teacher lived; and finally down the long kilometers to La Spezia, and, if you could fly, to the "Five

Lands" beyond, which could not be reached by car.

If you walked from the wharf to the alleys whose darkness beckons with ancient cooking and darting cats that might or might not have been ghosts, you would find yourself in Vecchia Lerici, Old Town, where the poorer villagers lived in their apartments, one of them Marco--the boy who would become my friend--and another, the strange girl who put spells on sea shells, making them dance on the sand for any boy she loved.

If you started walking from the bakery at beachside up the old brick path to Via San Giuseppe (where we lived in our tiny house), passed the dark convent where another poor friend lived, and left the road for the olive groves themselves, you would see the stone huts of the three witches. If you entered the groves with their feisty green lizards, you'd reach the brick path again, and in a few minutes the fork to tiny Magusa and its scarlet doorways, which you must avoid at all costs. If you walked on past the fork, panting at the climb, you would find at the top of the hill ten great villas built centuries before by Englishmen and aristocratic Italians, their gates--through which you could see endless Renaissance gardens unchanged by time — keeping everyone out, including upper class boys like you.

Beyond the villas, on the automobile road, you could walk to Sarzana and its musical festivals and then to the Seven Castle Towns — where, according to some legends, Satan had left his seven daughters to be raised by mortals--and, finally, down to the vineyard valley of the Magra River, to the marble face of Pisa and its silly, stubborn tower.

Here is the map I drew of Lerici one day after school, sitting in my bedroom, looking down through the olive trees at the sea, which sang to the village because the village sang to it, and always would. Later, I would make another map--one with colorful modeling clay — so that the green hills rose from a perfect blue sea and a little gray castle overlooked a cove with tiny fishing boats — and keep it in my bottom dresser drawer to look at whenever I wished.

No map, however--even the one inside us that guides our dreams each night--can hold the magic of the stories we have lived with our very breath.

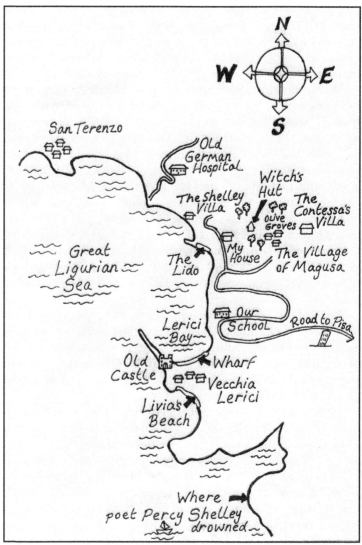

III

POISON

I'd just turned twelve. I accepted the magic because the village accepted it—because the people believed it. But magic isn't what makes us human. *Feelings* are; and I was barely aware of how much anger there was in my family, how it was my mother's way of keeping herself from sadness, from thinking about my baby brother too much, and how that anger traveled between us--between her and me, between her and my father, but never between me and my father--like an evil ping pong ball, or a ghostly cold, or something worse.

My mother was born a twin--there is that, too--and her twin brother died at birth. I often think her sadness began then, as if a piece of her were missing and always would be, as if she were incomplete without him—and without my brother. How to fill a hole like that except with anger?

On the day this story begins, I was happy enough. Thanks to my private tutor, *Dottore* Stellabotte, I'd done just as well as my friends Gianluca and Maurizio had on our Roman history recitation and the spelling test, which included the word *strega*—which meant *witch*—which could, if you weren't careful, get confused with *strage*, a massacre. Our teacher, *Professore* Brigola, had praised me, as he always did, when I passed the tests; and that had made me happy, too, and a little full of myself.

After school let out, my friends and I celebrated our good fortune by buying new plastic blowguns at the toy store in the fishing village and spending an hour making dozens of little paper cones with sewing needles taped to their points. Every boy had at least one blowgun—they were cheap—just two colorful plastic tubes and a handle—so I did too, of course.

When the cones were finished, we went back up the hill. There, on the convent wall--not far from my family's *villetta*— we hunted again the lizards that all boys in that country hunted:

The famous green "wall lizards" of Europe, *Podarcis muralis*, small but feisty creatures, their skin like green sandpaper, always ready to charge your shoes if they were angry at you, always ready to claim as theirs whatever Etruscan wall in the olive groves they chose. They were *daring* us to hunt them--that was obvious--but it wasn't easy hitting them. They weren't big, and they moved like lightning. To keep things equal, we stopped at six each, leaving the bodies—which made me sad if I looked at them too long--at the foot of the wall, where the convent cats might eat them if they were hungry enough.

The next night, after dinner, I watched my own cat--which I'd gotten that summer, slept with every night, and named "Nevis" (Latin for "snow")--die in my bathtub from the poison, making little lamb-like sounds until I couldn't stand it any longer. Helpless, I went outside to the flagstone patio to wait in darkness for the terrible noise to stop. When it did, I went back in, and saw it. The shadow.

It was hovering over the tub.

I held my breath until it was gone, and then picked up Nevis.

I believed what I'd seen—the shadow—because my friends often talked about things like that: The spells of *streghe*, the *ombre* of witches. But they also said, "Witches must eat"—which meant that, like kids and grown-ups, witches had to live in this world too. If they did something bad, they needed to face the consequences.

The body was limp, but still warm, and I cried. My parents were next door at our landlords, the Araldis, and wouldn't be back for a while. No one would hear me. No one would say, as my mother, her brown eyes flashing, sometimes did, "You're too attached to your pets, Brad. Even your dad thinks so."

I knew who'd done it. My friends would have said it even if I hadn't thought it. The three witches who lived in little shacks in the olive groves that covered the hills around our house always put out poison for cats. They didn't like cats. I knew this because--well, because everyone knew it. My friends talked about it because their families talked about it. I'd seen all three old women myself, more than once, walking through the olive groves. I'd even thrown vegetables at one of them--the tallest of the three--when Gianluca and Carlo started doing it one day on the road through the groves. We'd seen her in the trees, and she'd seen us, and she'd started shouting at us. If she hadn't, we wouldn't have thrown things, I don't think. One tomato hit her dress and made a mess, and that just made her shout more, dropping the bag of *funghi* she'd collected and storming off toward her shack, swearing in a dialect I knew I'd never understand.

If a cat died too suddenly in the hills for a doctor to help, and died in great pain, everyone knew it was poison and who'd put it out. It was what witches did--poisoning the animals you loved. Everyone in the village knew this, so I — I'd been there for five months already--knew it, too. There really were witches. If I'd had any doubt, that shadow over my bathtub had settled it. The shadow had been real. What I'd seen inside that shadow had been real.

Hand shaking, I found a paper bag under the kitchen sink just the right size for the body, put it in gently, twisted the top, and left it in the bathtub where no one would notice it during the night. It felt strange to do it, unkind and lonely, but it needed to be done — if I were to do what I needed to do. It was my bathroom, and no one would look in my tub until our maid came on Monday. If my parents asked where the cat was, I'd say I didn't know; and when I was finished with what needed to be done, I'd tell them what had happened. Or at least how the cat had died, poisoned by a witch, and where I'd buried her, which would be true by the time I was done.

The next morning, eating breakfast with my mother and father, I asked, "What do witches do on Sunday?"

"They're not witches," my mother answered, still in her angry mood, refusing to let sadness in. "They're just old women, Brad, and if they had family — if they lived in town with their families--the entire village would call them *befane*, Christmas witches, and not *streghe*, which is so unkind." My mother was a teacher, always teaching. She was smart--she had a master's degree and had taught for years--but she was wrong. They wouldn't be called *befane*. They'd be called *nonne — grandmothers-*-but she was frustrated she didn't know the language well enough to teach in this country, so she lectured whenever she could, right or wrong.

"It doesn't matter whether they're witches or not," I answered, and as I did, knew it had begun and that I couldn't turn back. *The truth. The courage to speak it. The anger needed for such courage*. To stand before the witch who'd done it and talk to her about what was fair and what wasn't, to make her feel what I felt. And by doing so, free myself from an anger that was like a spell, one that might hold me forever if I didn't find her in the olive groves and make her see what she had done.

"You could be more sensitive about the elderly," my mother was saying. "And you don't need to speak to me or your father in that tone of voice, Brad."

I have no tone of voice, I wanted to say, but knew this would only make her madder and I'd have to spend the morning undoing what I'd done. I had my own anger now, and anger was a powerful thing. It could give you courage. It could make people do what you wanted. But it was also a spell--like a song you couldn't get out of your head — and could make you a slave to it. I didn't want to be a slave to it, but I had a right to be angry, didn't I? My cat had died in my bathtub making terrible sounds; and as she'd died I'd stood there, watched it happen and seen the shadow: The soul of my cat being pulled from its dying body by the ghostly hand of an old woman, the end of her pinky finger missing.

I'll know the witch by her hand, I told myself again. *By her little finger….*

After breakfast, I went to my bathroom, picked up the paper bag carefully, and headed out into the olive grove toward the place where the trees, I remembered, were dead and the witches lived in their stone huts. My friends would have told me not to

--that only bad would come of it, "even if you are right to be sad and angry, Brad"--and I was surprised I was doing it. I was supposedly "shy." That's what people said. Why did it take the death of my cat for me to be brave? And was it really bravery? Or was it just the need to tell the truth--to stand before the old woman who did it and ask, "Why did you poison my cat?" but then to say, "I would not kill what you love, *Signora*."

I would begin, I decided, with the first stone hut, the one closest to my family's house on the hill. The witch who lived there would've found it easiest to poison my cat, wouldn't she? Whether she'd put the poison by her hut or in the olive trees nearer our house wouldn't have mattered. Nevis never went far, so her traveling to the huts of the two witches higher up the hill didn't make sense. It was the closest witch, I was sure. I never got a good look at her, but I heard her in her hut when my friends and I snuck in close one day, hiding in the little cave on the sunless side of the hill and watching from a distance, hoping to see her and yet scared. We never did see her, but we knew boys who had.

Her teeth, a boy from the wharf told us, were so bad you'd get nightmares if you looked at them. Yes, he'd seen her. Things were crawling in her mouth, and her tongue made a noise like a viper's hiss. Another boy, Claudio — one who lived near the castle that overlooked the bay--hadn't seen her himself, but his older brothers had, years ago. They'd seen her hut turn green, tremble as if it were alive, even move toward them, just before she looked up, saw them and shouted. They ran, and as they did, felt her green breath touch their backs. Days later they could still feel something crawling on them, and one of the brothers scratched himself bloody trying to stop the itch.

When I saw the hut through the trees, I stopped. It was green, sure, but that was because of the lichen. Everything in these groves — tree trunks, walls, and paths — had bright green lichen on it. And something moved, but it was only an olive branch scraping across the hut's thatched roof. The trees here weren't as dead-looking as I'd remembered them. They had leaves. They were very alive. Why I remembered them as dead, I didn't know, unless it was that fear had made it seem that way. I was not afraid today, so the trees were alive and the sunlight bright. Was that it?

There was a vegetable garden I didn't remember, and a stone path wandering from the hut's doorway into the grass, where it ended. I started toward it--under the trees, past a green lizard that watched me from a tree trunk, through the grass that reached my bare knees, through sudden yellow wildflowers, to the start of the path, its first flat stone, where I stopped. My heart jumped once in fear; but the sun was bright, and I clenched the paper bag, feeling courage.

"*Strega!*" I wanted to shout, because it was true, but instead I said courteously, with just a little anger, "*Signora!*"

No one appeared in the doorway, which seemed small — even for a witch. Now I shouted it:

"*Signora!*"

I rattled the bag a little. The body was stiff now, and I didn't want to shake it; but maybe the old woman, because she was a witch, would hear it and know the reason I was here — even if she wanted to ignore me.

"*Adesso!*" I said, rattling it again, wondering how long it took maggots to grow.

"*Devo parlarle, Signora!*" *I need to speak to you!*

Had Gianluca been with me, we would never come this close. We'd have stayed out under the nearest tree--or the second or third or fourth nearest--and thrown stones at the hut to get her attention, or shouted at her from a very safe distance. I was too angry for that, and anger could make you feel protected. Gianluca would let his own fear keep us in the trees, and the witch would know it, and it would give *her* courage — which I didn't want. Witches had enough as it was.

Besides, I wouldn't be able to see her hand if I stayed in the trees.

Something stirred in the darkness just inside the doorway,

as I'd known it would. *This is what witches do*, I told myself. They stir in the darkness--to scare you.

It was silly, the stirring. "Come out!" I shouted in her language. "I am here to do business with you. Have the courage to come out, *Signora!*"

Had I really shouted that in her language? Had I really known what words to use? Yes, because I heard myself shouting it again:

"*Venga qui! Coraggio, Signora!*"

After a moment the stirring spoke. "*Arrivo,*" it said, and the shadow stepped outside.

"*Cosa vuoi?*" she asked, annoyed, her teeth indeed terrible. Even at this distance they were little yellow sticks, gaps between them, and how she ate (if she did eat) I didn't know. Her hair was long and gray, and she was as hunched as I'd thought she'd be. But she was wearing black, as most old women in this country did, and this surprised me. The old women who wore black no longer had husbands, I knew. Their men were dead — from war, from heart attacks, from *fegato* problems--so they were widows, and widows wore black. But witches didn't have husbands. That's what Carlo had said more than once. "Witches never marry. They hate men and the boys who will become them!" A witch who wore black made no sense.

"I am here because of what is in this bag," I said, holding it up, trying to keep my hand from shaking. But it shook, and worse, I was too far from her for my plan to work. I'd have to be close enough that with just one step she could take the bag from me--to look inside--and when she did, I'd see her hand.

I took a step toward her, stopped, took another, holding the bag out. No matter what I did--no matter how much anger I made myself feel--my hand would not stop shaking. Maybe it wasn't fear? Maybe it was anger that made it shake?

When I was at last in front of her, I tried not to look at her teeth, but at her eyes--which were nearly closed, as if afraid of the light. If I stared at her eyes — if I made her feel my anger — perhaps the shaking would stop.

But then I smelled her. It was the smell of old women--old women at the Saturday market in town, old women on the wharf (when they didn't smell like fish), and also the smell of my own grandmother, my father's mother, when I was little, before she died. It was the smell of vinegar — "She uses it on her hair," my mother used to say. I'd loved my grandmother, but there were other smells to this old woman, too, and they were not my grandmother's.

Her eyes opened a little then, and I saw that one was brown and one was green. This didn't surprise me. Witches weren't like ordinary people.

I was wrinkling my nose at her smell, I knew, and before I could stop she said:

"Do not come close if my body offends you, *ragazzo*."

My courage weakened, and for a moment I couldn't find the anger.

"I am not here, *Signora*," I said quickly as I could, "to discuss smells. I am here about what it is in this bag."

I thrust it at her. When she didn't take it, I held my hand as steady as I could and waited. If I couldn't see her hand, I wouldn't know!

When she spoke, I wasn't sure I'd heard her correctly.

"You wish to see my hand?" she repeated.

The bag was shaking even more now, but I made myself nod. "Yes, I wish to see your hand."

She made a sound like a snort, reached out and grabbed the bag. As she did, she shifted her weight to her other leg, which was shorter and even skinnier. For a moment I thought she might fall, and if she did, what would I do then? Should you touch a witch? Should you help her up?

But she didn't fall. She steadied herself, holding the bag in her hand, and stared at me. I still hadn't seen her hand, but I had to look away. Her eyes *knew* me — my bedroom, my cat, my parents' house — and the knowing made me afraid.

"I know what this bag holds, *ragazzo*. I do not need to look inside it. What dies deserves respect. Not to be put in a bag--not to be opened in the sunlight and stared at. Do you not agree?"

"Yes," I said, and then I saw it. The green lichen that covered, completely covered, the hut—its walls and thatch roof--was beginning to move. All of it. To wiggle. No, not wiggle, but to crawl, moving towards us slowly even as I felt myself stop breathing. The hut was moving. No—the *lichen* was.

But it wasn't lichen. It was--

Lizards.

It wasn't possible. *Lizards*. Hundreds—maybe thousands— of them. The green lizards that lived in these groves were all here somehow, sunning themselves on the roof and sunlit side of the hut, and now leaving their sunny places to move toward the old woman and me.

They were hers, I knew then.

They were her pets.

They were coming to see what a boy might want with their mistress.

And then the movement stopped, and the roof and side of the hut fell still again.

The lizards were waiting, I could see—but for what?

It was like a dream, but it wasn't. It was real. She was a witch, after all, and with a witch anything was possible.

"Then why did you put what you loved--and what loved you--in a bag?" she was asking me, holding it but not looking in it.

I made myself find the words I'd practiced.

"Because I wanted you to see it."

"Why?"

"Because I was angry."

"Why?"

"Because I knew that someone poisoned her. I saw the hand that did it. I wanted the person to see what she had done."

The old woman didn't speak for a moment.

"Like all boys," she said at last with a sigh, "you understand nothing. But here is my hand, *ragazzo*."

Holding the bag, the hand came toward me, stopping so

27

close to my face that I had to step back.

When a lizard crawled suddenly from the old woman's black sleeve, I almost screamed. The old woman snorted again and the lizard scampered down the side of the bag and back up to her hand.

"*Via!*" she said to it. The creature returned to her sleeve, where three others were peering out now, watching me.

"Is this the hand you saw?"

It was. Two blue veins made a Y, with the end of the pinky finger missing, just as it had in the bathroom.

I nodded.

The old woman said nothing. It was up to me.

"Why did you want the soul of the animal I loved?" I asked.

When she spoke at last, it was with another sigh.

"It was not the soul of your cat I took," she said. I didn't want it to, but it sounded true, and because it did, my anger left me again and with it my courage.

"I was taking *another* thing," she was saying, or at least that is what I heard. Whether she was actually speaking the words— out loud, in the air, in this sunlight--I couldn't be sure. I didn't hear words in her language. I heard my own language and I couldn't even be sure she was speaking at all--with a throat. "I was taking back," her voice was saying, "the soul of my *lucertola*--my lizard."

It didn't make sense. My cat was not a lizard. But then I understood--because she wished me to: *My cat had eaten a lizard, and it had been one of hers. My cat had ventured into the grove too far, come upon her hut and her lizards, and, as cats do, eaten one of them.*

It was true. It was not some lie she wanted me to believe.

She had poisoned my cat because my cat had killed her lizard? She had lost something she had loved, too, and had acted in anger?

I could've said, "Was *poison* the only way?"

But then she would say, "I chased your cat away many times, but she kept coming back, curious, ready to eat more of my lizards if I did not poison her."

I could say, "Why didn't you come to my house and tell me? You knew where I lived."

Then she would say, "You would have wanted a witch in your doorway? You would have believed her? You would not, in anger, have come with your friends to throw rocks at her house?"

Worst of all, she might say, "I killed what you loved to save what I love," and what would my answer be then—except the silence of sadness? She was a witch and might be lying—to make me go away—but it would not feel like a lie, and so I would have no words.

Before I could say anything at all, the old woman—eyes on me, bag in her hand, the four lizards still peeking at me from her sleeve—said, "I know where you live, yes, but I could not have come to you. I cannot go far from my house because— because of them." She gestured at the lizards. "But that is not the point of this. The point is that I did not poison your cat."

Now she was lying. I was sure of it. Witches did lie. They said and did what they needed to do and say to get what they wanted--to trip people up-- especially children. They hated the happiness and lives of ordinary people—and "They hate the innocence of children," Carlo's mother had told us at dinner once--so they did whatever they could to trick you, to hurt you. It had been this way forever. World without end.

"My cat was poisoned," I said.

"Yes," the old woman answered, "but it was not poison."

"What?"

"Your cat came to these trees and ate my lizard."

"So?"

"My lizard was the poison."

"I do not understand you."

"My lizards are not ordinary lizards, and because they are not, they are poison to anything that eats them."

She was playing more tricks now. She was saying whatever she needed to say to make me lose my courage forever. It was like a spell, one that used logic to confuse the mind — to take away confidence. I could feel myself spinning within it, the spell, like a moth in a spider's cocoon.

I wanted to run, but couldn't. I needed the bag back. How could I leave without it?

"You are putting a spell on me," I said, as if saying it might change it.

"Words have no power," she answered, "which you do not give them."

This was true. I had thought this myself when my mother, in an anger she wouldn't let go of, used words that made me feel shame. Without her words, I knew, there could be no shame.

"That is true," I found myself saying, not wanting to, but saying it anyway; and when I did, she made a little smile with her mouth. It was both wonderful and horrible. The little sticks showed against the dark hole of her mouth, and the skin of her lips pulled tight, like a corpse's skull, cracking. Little lines of blood appeared in the cracks, but the smile didn't give up. It stayed.

If it was a spell I was feeling, it wasn't a bad one.

"What are they," I asked suddenly, "if they are not lizards?"

After another snort, she said:

"They are what is left of the man I loved."

As I stared at her black dress, the one so many old women in this country wore, I knew this was true, too.

As if tired from smiling, she frowned, but said quietly:

"Come in."

This was how the story always went, wasn't it? The witch would get the boy or girl inside her hut, and that would be the end of it. As Terotto had told us once, a witch's spells are more powerful where she lives--in her own hut--where, like her smell or breath or bony hand, they're a part of her and have her power. She needed to get me inside to do what she wanted to me. Any witch would. The gentleness of her words was a lie, wasn't it?

"I cannot make you enter," she said. "I can only invite you in."

This had to be a trick. This kindness; this honesty; this pretending she didn't have the power, the spells, to *make* me do what she wanted. "A witch," Fabio had told us, "will tell you anything she needs to tell you." Fabio knew because his own uncle had been killed by a witch's spell during the war. "With a lie she got him to sit beside her on a bench in the old cemetery, telling him she was there to grieve her sister. She touched his hand just once, but it was enough to put it on him. Fifteen days later he died in his bed like a dog!"

She was offering me the bag now. I could leave if I wanted to.

"If you will not come in, you should have your cat back, to bury it as you wish, to say a blessing over it because it was something you loved."

This was not how witches were supposed to talk — this kindness. It was more trickery. It had to be. I should grab the bag and leave before she changed her mind.

But as I took the bag from her, the lizards in her sleeve scampered down her arm and onto mine. I jumped and started to turn — to run — but she was looking at me with her one brown eye and her one green eye, and the lizards felt good. They scampered down my arm again, back up, and stopped, watching me. I couldn't look away. They were green and beautiful and they seemed to like me. If they were a trick, they weren't a trick from any story I'd ever heard. They weren't howling black cats or screeching owls or hissing vipers, the pets witches were known for. They were green and cheerful, and I was sorry I'd ever killed the lizards of this country.

As I looked at the ones on my arm, the walls and roof of the hut began moving again like a slow green wave. They flowed like water down the path, under the old woman's feet, around them, to my own sandals. For a moment I jerked in fear, but their toes and tails on my bare legs tickled, so I smiled.

When the wave stopped at last, I was covered with them. My

arms and legs and shorts and shirt were green. I itched, sure, but it was fine.

"Come in," she said again; and, walking carefully so as not to knock any of them from me, I followed her into the hut.

As I stood in the darkness with her, she touched my arm lightly, and I didn't jump. She whistled once, as if calling a dog, but it was a witch's whistle — not just a sound in the air, for ears, but something more. As she whistled, a green light swirled like fog from her mouth, and the lizards that had followed us in, their tiny faces faintly lit by the dim glow from her mouth, looked up at her from the floor.

She had begun to whisper, too, and it sounded like *"Ricordatevelo"* — *"Remember him"*--and the lizards, in the light of the fog, their eyes like green stars, began to move toward the dark center of the room.

Beside me her voice said, "Can you see our bed?"

I could. In the dim green light I could see, in the middle of the floor, what looked like blankets, heavy wool ones, lying on a piece of lumpy canvas. What was inside the canvas, I didn't know. Straw, rags, old clothes –anything to fill it. The bed was on the floor, and, except for blankets, it was empty. That was obvious. But the lizards were gathering there; and as I looked at the green shadow that was the bed, it started to change. It was empty, but *something* was taking shape there.

The lizards on my arms and legs moved and then fell still. I took a breath.

"This is where we slept when the war was over."

"Yes," I heard myself say, and a lizard moved from my neck to my ear.

"We lived here because we were poor," she was saying, though in what language I wasn't sure. "My husband, whose name was Pagano Lorenzo, picked grapes at Bocca di Magra. That was what he did."

"Yes," I said again.

"Do you see him?"

"What?"

"My husband?"

"No...."

"That is because my sister, who lives in Vernazza, killed him. She did not have a man. Her man, whom she did not really love, died at Ancona in the war, while mine returned. She hated me for my fortune and one day asked us to dinner. She prepared *dateri*, using the largest clams, and the portion she gave him was poisoned. It is easy to do if you know *stregoneria*, if you are *strega*. You could poison your sister in jealousy — or at least try, witch to witch--but why bother? Why not instead take away what she loves, what you yourself do not have, so that you can watch her sadness forever? Do you see him now, *ragazzo*?"

I was shaking again. I blinked, brushing a lizard's tail from my eye. I could see that the shadow on the bed was bigger now. I could feel the lizards on my arms and legs leaving me to join the others on the bed, where the shadow kept growing.

"I — I..."

"Boys who tell stories about us do not understand. We cannot do *everything*. I could not save my husband. He died on this bed from the poison, the kind used for rats. He died in great pain. With a spell she blinded his tongue to the taste of it and he ate it all."

The shadow on the bed was darkening, and I could not stop shaking now.

"I did what I could, *ragazzo*. The lizards of these groves felt for us the affection we felt for them. They had lived with us, and we with them; and so, when my husband died, I gave his soul to them--a piece to each — a thousand pieces...."

I was shaking so hard I could barely stand. The shadow on the bed was complete now, and the old woman, though her legs and hip seemed to hurt her, stepped to the window to open it. As sunlight fell to the bed, I saw what the lizards had made with their bodies, the shape of it: A man, sleeping peacefully on his stomach, green as lichen in the sunlight, but one that in the night might be as real as a man needed to be for his wife, with her memories, to fall asleep.

She'd wanted the piece of him back. That was all. I could see it now. She hadn't poisoned my cat. Her lizard had. The lizard that was a piece of her husband's poisoned soul.

"I sleep well at night," the old woman was saying, "because we sleep well when we sleep with what we love. How do you sleep, *ragazzo*?"

As I walked back through the groves to my house, the bag heavy in my hand, I thought about Nevis, and missed her. I could hear the grass rustling behind me. How many there were, I didn't know. A hundred perhaps, maybe more. I wanted to look, but I also didn't want to scare them away. Even when I reached the steps to our house, I didn't look back. I got a shovel from the shed, returned to the nearest trees, and, taking a deep breath, dug a hole where my parents couldn't see me digging. I buried the body there, saying a blessing as I filled the hole with dirt. I used the Lord's Prayer because I'd used it before--when my pets had died--but also because I didn't know any other. They waited in the grass while I did this. Then I went back to the house, to my room—stepping quietly past the kitchen and my mother's anger, which did not have to be mine anymore—and saw how it would go: I'd open my bedroom window just enough so that they could enter when they wanted to, sunning themselves on the windowsill and coming inside when the sun had set. At night—any night I wished it—all I needed to do was lie on my bed, whisper *"Remember her"* to the darkness. Then I'd wait while the tiny feet and tails moved over me and the animal I'd loved--the one I'd slept with every night for three months--took shape beside me, paws tucked neatly under her, her body somehow warm, so I could fall asleep at last.

IV

OMBRA

It was just a house the American boy and his family lived in, but the people of the fishing village called it a villetta. The owner, a Dr. Araldi who lived in a real villa higher on the hill--not far from the Villa Musetti and the Villa Tincani with their endless gardens--called it a villetta, too: Villetta la Lupetta. Little Villa of the Little Wolf. It was a simple two-story stucco house, but it was a little villa to those who didn't live on the hillside overlooking the blue-water cove and the village, who lived in apartments instead, the dark ones in the old part of town or the sunnier ones on the streets leading to the main highway that wound through the seven castle towns and then on to Pisa with its famous tower.

None of the boy's friends--the ones he'd gotten to know the first summer he was there, before school started--lived near him, except one, Giacomo, who was also the poorest. There was an apartment attached to the convent at the end of Via San Giuseppe, the dirt road that led from the hillside villas to the main streets of the village, and there Giacomo lived with his family. His apartment was even darker than the ones in Old Lerici with its wet alleys and scraggly cats. It amazed the American boy (and bothered some of his friends) that a family with so little--a "technical-school family of no means"--could live on the hillside with the wealthy; but he was glad it was Giacomo's family that did.

Years later the American boy would not remember how they first met, he and Giacomo. He would remember, as if in snapshots, his skinny friend standing at the end of Via San Giuseppe waving to him all those afternoons, shouting for him to join him. He would remember, too, the last time he saw his friend on the road, standing at the bottom of the villetta's steps, not coming any closer, the green lizards peering at them from the wall. He would of course remember what had happened: The miracle of Giacomo's grandmother, standing up at last on her dirty mattress in the dark room, no longer coughing, the cross glowing on the wall--glowing like a little sun. It had happened when

35

he went to his friend's apartment the last time, only weeks before he and his family had to leave the village and return to their world. Though it made no sense, these memories were in shadow, as if they had happened at dusk, or on an overcast day. The first time they had met would have been bright--without shadow--for innocence, he now knew, was a light which, though it might be misplaced, could not really be lost....

V

THE BLEEDING CHILD

It was the Cold War—Communism against the West--and my father was stationed in that country to help fight the Cold War quietly, the way it was almost always fought. My friends from school in the village where we would live for those three years weren't afraid, of course. It wasn't like a real war. There were no planes at night, no bombs, no radio announcements of impending invasions, and no wounded, bleeding men—nothing like the war their parents had fought in countless villages fifteen years earlier. There were young people dancing to popular songs at night at the *lido*, the dance club in the next cove, and we could hear the songs from our bedroom windows. There were movies to see—*Maciste* sword-and-sandal epics and silly comedies—at the little theater across from the school. These were *not* the sounds and scenes of war. Except for my own parents' occasional mention of "nuclear missiles" and "the communist threat," I wasn't afraid either. Why would I be? I was thirteen. We all were thirteen—young, innocent and trusting. We went about our business, which was the business of growing up. What could there possibly be to scare us?

There was one thing, though, that frightened my friends— frightened them much more than witches--and it was something that had nothing at all to do with war. It was the cobblestone path that led from our village, little Lerici with its medieval church and castle, up through the olive groves of the witches to the hilltop where the villas of the old aristocratic families overlooked the Ligurian Sea. My friends, all born in Lerici, were scared of that path, and admitted it. It wasn't that you couldn't stay on the path and avoid the fork that took you to the even tinier village of Magusa halfway up the hill. It was that when the path did fork, you felt the strange pull of Magusa's olive groves and doorways with their red hammers and sickles (or what looked like hammers and sickles), and it felt like a spell, a trick of magic, one that left you feeling a little sick. That's how my friends put it anyway, loving the drama of it.

The grownups saw it differently. Magusa was a communist village, they said—if you could call something that small a village—and a communist village angrier than most; and that (the grownups declared) was all you needed to know. Lots of people in Italy were communists—churchgoing, card-carrying communists who had no trouble believing both in God and the rights of the working man, of common people shortchanged by the aristocracy for far too long--but the residents of Magusa were different: They were communists *so* poor and so angry with the world that their comrades in other villages, no strangers to red bandanas and shouting crowds, didn't want to be around them. The residents of Magusa weren't even from Liguria, the grownups said. The original families, all olive pickers, had come from the farthest south. They looked like Southerners, too—short and darker--and that didn't help. Northerners had always looked down on Southerners, and always would. Or, as the grownups put it, the villagers of Magusa had never really "adjusted" to being *Ligurians*.

But my friends knew better, they told me after school one day, staying late enough that they might have seen the lizards coming through my bedroom window if I hadn't guided them downstairs to tell them goodbye.

Sure (my friends said), the doorways of Magusa were short, which said Southerners perhaps, and certainly said poor. The houses, lined up side by side and touching on both sides of a cobblestone path no more than a few meters wide, were narrow and dark and damp, and the doorways were shorter than most men. But this wasn't, my friends insisted, because the villagers of Magusa were small, though they were indeed squat and small. *It was because the villagers wanted to keep something out— out of their houses--something bigger than men.*

And though (my friends insisted) the bright scarlet slashes of paint on every door did indeed look a little like hammers and

sickles — those symbols of communism you always heard about-
-they really weren't hammers and sickles at all. They were
something else, something much stranger.

Maybe the inhabitants of Magusa were communists, they
said, and maybe they weren't. What mattered was not what the
crude design in red paint on every doorway "represented," they
said, but what it *did*.

"*Che dice?*" I said. "What do you mean 'did'?"

"The doorways aren't enough," Gianluca, my best friend —
the one with the long eyelashes who dreamed of working for
Interpol when he grew up--said quietly. I was trying to get my
friends to take the fork to Magusa that day because it was the
shortest route by far to the *trattoria* in Romito — the one that had
the best ice cream on the coast — and I was in a mood for ice
cream. We were bored as hell that afternoon, our geography and
Roman history tests behind us, and ice cream was — in my case
anyway — going to break the boredom. They'd argued with
me — saying that the gelato at Trattoria Mitiale or del Golfo on
the waterfront was better — but I knew they just didn't want to
walk all that way, especially if it meant going through Magusa.

"They've got the best *panna cotta*," I'd said, "and you know
it. You're just scared."

"No," blue-eyed Maurizio had said, turning red the way he
always did when he lied. "We just don't want to walk to Romito
for your damn ice cream."

No one uttered a word for a moment, and then Gianluca said
what they were all feeling:

"We don't want you to go alone."

Carlo, always the bravest and cockiest, snorted, and said,
"Speak for yourself, Gianluca."

"I do, Carlo."

Carlo snorted again, but didn't say anything else.

"Why not?" I asked. I knew, but wanted them to say it. I
didn't believe it, and I wanted to give them a hard time.

"You know why," Maurizio said shyly.

"All of this — everything you've told me before about

39

Magusa," I began, "you have gotten from adults who know?"

"No…." Maurizio said.

"You have imagined it, then?" I was still sleeping with the lizards each night, but I was certainly not going to tell my friends about them.

"No!" Gianluca frowned. "We have put it together, like detectives. We have lived here longer than you and we have had time to do detective work."

Gianluca's boast embarrassed Carlo, who looked away, but still said nothing.

"Just the three of you — you three detectives?" I teased.

"Of course not," Carlo said suddenly. "The calculations began with my uncle, Paolo, who is twenty years older. He started, with his friends, to put two and two together when he was young; and my brother, Emiliano, who is ten years older, did the same. The detective work, if you want to call it that, has been accumulating for at least twenty years, Brad."

"And how do boys know what adults do not?" I asked, a part of me *wanting* to believe, but the rest not wanting to be a fool. Why did getting ice cream have to be so complicated?

Gianluca took the condescending tone he sometimes did — the one you wanted to shoot him for, even if he was your best friend. "You are so simple, Brad. You are an American and do not understand such things."

"Yes," Carlo agreed. "You are like the adults who want to think what they want to think, and so they do not really think. They do not use their brains." Carlo was a little older, had the highest grades in our subjects and would be an attorney some day, we knew--maybe even city attorney of La Spezia, the port to the north.

"They do not," he went on, "really want to discover the truth."

"And so," Gianluca added, "they do not explore; they do not bother to find out — to find out important *things*."

This was getting ridiculous. "Things? Like what?"

"Like a baby crying in the night," Carlo answered.

"What's strange about that?"

My friends didn't answer. They were looking at each other now.

"This baby cries in Magusa," Carlo answered.

"There's a crying baby in *any* village," I responded, exasperated. Could this get any sillier?

"But we've all heard it," Maurizio was saying.

"So?"

"It's just one baby," Maurizio went on, "and when it cries, it doesn't stop." He was staring at me, pleading, as if to say: *Please believe us. I would not lie to you, Brad.*

And he wouldn't.

"When?"

"In the night."

"It can't just be one baby."

"But it is," Carlo insisted. "We recognized it. There are no other voices, no people, no children, no other babies. Just this one and it cries all night."

I didn't know what to say. I'd gotten a shiver, the way Carlo was telling it, but that just made me mad because I knew he *wanted* me to shiver. He loved to scare people. He'd learned it from his dad, who'd have a glass of wine and off he'd go with a ghost story until the women told him to stop. "You're scaring us all, Bruno, so *zito*, please!"

"So you heard it, Carlo—"

"Yes, he did," said Gianluca. "We all did."

"How?"

"Before you and your family came to live here," Gianluca said. "Maybe two years ago. We went to Magusa, we took the fork, we stayed in the groves until night, and we waited. We had flashlights. We wanted to explore the village at night, using flashlights, but suddenly we were scared. Something scared us and we stayed in the trees all night."

"We thought dogs would smell us or hear us and we'd have to run," Maurizio said.

"*But they don't have dogs,*" Gianluca said.

41

"What?"

"*They don't,*" Gianluca said again, "*have dogs.*"

"You've never heard dogs barking at Magusa?"

"No."

"No one has. Ever."

"Even the adults say they haven't. They think it strange, but not strange enough to change how they think."

"*Bene.* I agree," I said, "that's strange, but a baby crying isn't strange. You're trying to make that village stranger than it is because you just don't want to walk to Romito."

"No," Maurizio said quietly. That Maurizio believed it — that was what was most persuasive of all. He was the clearest thinker in school, the calmest, the kindest, the most reasonable; and if *he* believed…. I felt a chill again.

"There was just that one infant," Gianluca insisted.

"I doubt that a village has just one baby," I said, repeating myself, but not wanting to give up that easily. Finding a thing unbelievable was not the same as being afraid to believe it, I knew.

"We stayed," he went on, "in the bushes until after midnight. We knew we would get in trouble with our parents, but we were--"

"You, Gian, were afraid to move even a centimeter," Carlo interrupted smugly.

"So were you!" Gianluca glared at him.

Carlo said nothing.

Gianluca calmed down, looked at me and went on.

"All we could do was listen to that baby cry."

"Until after midnight?"

"Yes….all that time."

"How many hours?"

"Six, maybe a little more."

"I don't believe you sat in the bushes not moving for six hours."

"We do not lie, Brad," Maurizio said.

"You didn't have to go to the bathroom?"

"We went to the bathroom."

"Right there? In the bushes?"

"Yes."

"Why?"

"Because we had to go...but we couldn't leave."

I was staring at the three of them, looking for any sign on their faces that it was a joke. There was nothing. "Mary Mother of God," I said. "You are all crazy. You scared yourselves. You scared each other. You couldn't even *move*? You went in the grass where you were hiding?"

They looked at me for a second, and it was Maurizio who spoke:

"You wouldn't have been able to move either."

"Why?"

"Because it was as if the baby were alone—that's what its crying sounded like--as if no one were there to hold it or nurse it--as if all of the people in the village were gone and only the baby was there alone—as if....." Maurizio ran out of words, and his mouth hung open for a moment.

"Just one baby—you're sure?"

"Yes."

"No adult voices?"

Gianluca sighed. "No adult voices anywhere."

They were standing on the path with me, and we were all silent. I'd run out of questions and they'd run out of answers. I believed them, I suppose—enough that I was still feeling the whisper of a chill—but I sure had no idea what it meant.

"So...let's go," I said.

"What?" they said. It was the exact opposite of what they wanted to hear. I was supposed to be scared now. I was supposed to want to go anywhere *but* Magusa.

"Let's take the fork," I went on. "Let's find out what it means. It's daytime. There are four of us. What do we have to be afraid of?"

They'd all stepped back as if I'd sprayed them with a hose. I know why I said it. I was angry. I was angry that they'd

43

scared me with their story, and I wanted to get back at them. I didn't really want to go to Magusa now, and they didn't either, so the last thing I expected was Carlo's next words:

"*Va bene.* Let's go."

"What?" Now it was my turn.

"You're right, Brad. The time to go there is daytime, when there are as many of us as possible. Besides...."

I didn't know what the "besides" meant, but the others did. "Besides?"

"You're an American, and that may protect us."

"If they're communists," I countered, "they certainly won't want to see an American."

"Maybe," Carlo said. "*If* they're communists. But what may protect us—"

The others were nodding now, as if they'd all talked about it.

"—is your red hair. If they are, as our parents say, from the South, that should frighten them. *Barbarossa.* The devil's beard. The evil eye. It wouldn't frighten Northerners because they have red hair sometimes—look at Armando--but if they're Southerners, maybe they'll think you're the devil."

I wanted to say, *And what if they are the devil?*, but didn't. I was suddenly very self-conscious of my hair.

"*We* don't think you're the devil," Gianluca said, as if I needed the assurance. "But Carlo is right--maybe *they* will."

Again I thought they were joking—how could they say such a thing with a straight face?—but they weren't smiling, they weren't laughing.

"It should," Carlo added somberly, like an old priest, "give you power over them."

"It is daylight, too," little Maurizio added brightly, "so they will see your hair better."

I wanted to laugh--to break the tension and help me breathe--but the idea of laughing was somehow scary, too.

So we did it. We took the fork. Our hearts were beating louder than our footsteps on the cobbles—at least mine was--and we kept scanning the shadows of the olive groves on either side of us like soldiers looking for an enemy. The cobbles on the fork were rougher, and we tripped a lot, our eyes on the trees where things could hide, watching us. No one said a thing, as if speaking would bring the shadows to life, and it took an hour to reach the village when it should have taken half that.

I looked at innocent Maurizio, he looked back, and I knew what he was thinking: *See how much sunlight there is here, Brad! They'll be able to see your red hair perfectly. It almost glows!*

The village was about a block long. There were no lizards on the walls. No one was on the path that led through it, or in the doorways that lined it. No voices reached us from anywhere-- houses or olive groves beyond them. No one was there to watch us arrive, and no one appeared as we walked past the doorways with their red paint. I had walked this path once before, with my parents, not long after we'd arrived in Lerici, and there had been no lizards or people then either. We'd been taking a Sunday walk to the Villa Musetti on the ridge to say hello to the Contessa, who'd befriended my mother in our first weeks in the country—as the aristocracy of any country tends to do with military officers, who are, after all, the military's own aristocracy—and we'd taken the Magusa fork by accident. I hadn't paid much attention. I was chubbier then, completely out of shape, and walking that far uphill had winded me. I saw the red paint and knew what hammers and sickles were, so when my father pointed them out, calling them just that, I nodded. Then he said, "Have we been here before?" and my mother said, "No, Charles, we haven't. And I'm really not sure we should be here." "I'm not sure either," he answered quickly. Their instant of fear made me afraid, too. An American family—a symbol of oppression, as the newspapers put it, to the downtrodden here—should not be wandering into a little village so off the beaten track and so full, we knew, of ardent communists. It wasn't that I really thought the townspeople would hurt us, clubs or knives or fists or anything like that. It was simply that

I didn't want to be screamed at, which had already happened to us on a bus tour in Rome; but I also didn't want to insult them, by walking where I shouldn't walk. Their lives were hard. You could tell that from the tiny, dark and damp houses they lived in. You could tell from the size of their doorways. If you're a symbol of wealth and power—something they'd never had and never would have—why would you want to rub it in, parading up their cobblestone path, a red-haired boy, a tall blue-eyed father of military bearing, a pretty mother in a nice dress, all three so very American? If you did that, maybe you *deserved* to be shouted at, I told myself.

That day with my parents no one had come out of the houses either. It had been a Sunday afternoon and no one would be in the groves picking olives or pruning the trees or weeding under them; and yet no one was on the path or in the doorways. *What a strange little town*, I thought, but nothing more. When we mentioned it later to my tutor—that we had taken that path by accident—the *Dottore*, a dignified man from La Spezia who held his cigarettes tightly, as if they might somehow escape him, said, "Please do not do that again, *Capitano*. That is not an appropriate place for an officer and his family--American or Italian." Even he did not seem to feel it had been that dangerous an outing—only that Magusa was a place where upper-class people should not, by propriety, go. No more than that. No more dangerous than Naples in daylight. Just common sense—common sense in a world where social classes did not always get along, *Capitano*.

As my three friends and I walked through the village now, the hammers and sickles didn't look much like hammers and sickles at all. About that my friends had been right. The crude design looked more like a big crescent moon with a cross slapped over it. At first I told myself it had been easier, faster, for whoever had painted them to do it this way: You make a crescent for the sickle, leave off the handle, and paint the hammer so fast it looks like a cross. Everyone will still know what it is, right? But as we walked on, I saw that every doorway had it *exactly* the same—

sickle without a handle, ends tapering like a crescent moon, and the cross definitely a cross.

Some of the designs were large, some small, and couldn't have been made by the same person; and yet the design was always the same: Crescent moon and cross.

"You're right," I said at last. "Those aren't hammers and sickles."

"Of course not," Carlo answered proudly, as if I were complimenting him.

A sound farther up the path made us freeze.

Where the last houses were on the path, just up ahead, a door had started to open. My heart jumped, and I knew what the others were thinking because I was thinking it too: *Now it's going to happen. Someone is going to step from a house and start screaming at us – but isn't that better than what we'd imagined?*

But it didn't happen. Instead, from the doorway a head peered out. It was too far away to see whether it was man or woman, and it peered at us for a second even as a hand reached down to pick something up from the cobbles in front of the doorway. Then the hand stopped, withdrew, the head disappeared, and the door closed.

When the door stayed closed, we started walking again, and when we reached the front of that doorway, slowed. There, on the cobbles, was a bucket, and inside it, paint, red paint, the surface starting to harden, the paint separating into different fluids. That's what it looked like anyway as we reached the bucket, looked down in it, and found ourselves stopping to stare. We didn't want to stop. We didn't want the person inside the house to step out and start screaming at us – "Who do you think you are, *ragazzi maleducati*, sons of engineers and draftsmen, children of privilege! – with an American boy with you as well!"--but we couldn't stop looking at the paint. It was obviously the paint they used on the doors. It was what they used to make the hammers and sickles that weren't hammers and sickles at all.

Carlo, always the bravest of us, or the most full of bravado, was leaning, actually leaning, over the bucket to get a good look, saying, "What is that?"

"What is what?" I said. I could see inside the bucket from where I stood, but I certainly wasn't going to get as close as Carlo was to it.

"*That,*" he said, pointing at the paint.

We looked in all directions to make sure we were safe, and then, as if given permission by God or someone, crowded around the bucket.

There were three layers of fluid in the bucket. There was the bright red paint, but also two layers on top of that—one a clear, yellowish fluid, like what comes from a cut on your finger, and the other a clotted material that was red, sitting in clumps on the paint below it.

We all stepped back, even Carlo. *Not everything in that bucket is paint*, we were thinking. *But if it isn't paint....*

In the bucket was a stick—from an olive tree—one that had been used to mix the paint and that was covered with all three--yellow fluid, dark clots, bright red paint.

"That's blood," Carlo said, sure of himself.

No one argued.

Carlo moved suddenly and we all jumped. He was reaching down with his right hand and with his index finger touching it.

"Are you *pazzo?*" Gianluca whispered hoarsely, taking another step back, as if the bucket were going to explode and we'd all be covered with what was in it. "That's blood, Carlo!"

"I know, *idiota,*" Carlo answered. He had touched the dark clots and was raising his finger to look at it. Carlo might have been the bravest of us, but he also needed to make sure we knew it—and sometimes this made him do stupid things.

"Wipe it off! Wipe it off!" Gianluca was whispering.

"Why?"

"Because—because—"

Carlo was smelling his fingertip now, and I was ready to scream, too, it was so close to his face, his eyes, his mouth.

"Wipe it off," I said. "Please, Carlo. We know you're brave."

This annoyed him. He glared at me.

"Don't you want to be brave, too?" he asked.

"No…." I said.

He started to wipe it on his shorts and Gianluca grabbed his arm. "Not your shorts!"

He wiped it instead on the lip of the bucket, and, as he did, the door opened. We didn't even look. We just started running.

You'd think it would take a shouting voice to make you run faster, but that day in Magusa it was the silence of whoever stood in that doorway behind us — someone we never turned to see--that made us run faster. *Just one baby crying in the night*, I remember thinking as I ran. *No one there on a Sunday…no one ever there…hammers and sickles that were moons and crosses…buckets that held more than paint….*

On a crumbling wall at the village's end there was a lizard at last, and as we ran past it I wondered whether it was one of the ones that slept with me each night.

Yes, it answered, but that was impossible.

I heard later from Gianluca that Carlo developed a rash on his hand — the hand that had touched what was in the bucket-- but who knows whether that was true. Carlo was always putting his nose (and his hands) where they didn't belong. All I know is that we ran as hard as we did from Magusa that day — on to Romito and ice cream that wasn't so great after all---because of the silence and a baby we never even heard.

It never occurred to me that the village of red paint would get me to return — and return alone — for a dog.

When Magusa called again, I was a year older, and, I liked to think, tougher — the way that life's lessons make you tougher. I'd confronted the witch I thought had poisoned my cat and learned about anger. I'd stood up for a working-class friend, Giacomo — whose family lived in a dark, tiny apartment attached to the convent down the road from us — against both my tutor's snobbery and the merciless teasing of technical-school boys; and because I had, I'd seen magic in the way the little cross made of braided twigs on my friend's wall glowed until the bullying stopped, and his grandmother, an invalid, standing up in the same glow and walking one day on legs that hadn't worked in years. I was also now as good as my dad at consoling my mother when she thought too much about my brother and was feeling her darkness, when her eyes were like shadows. Her crying no longer scared me. I was able to give her what light I could—that is what love is, isn't it?--a light we give?--and sometimes it was enough.

And of course, if you wanted more proof, the witch's lizards no longer slept with me. I didn't need them anymore, which they and their mistress understood; and so, one night, they'd left me and I was not as lonely as I thought I'd be.

In other words, I'd grown up a lot in a year, or at least told myself I had; and if I was older and had grown up a lot, I must be tougher--and if I was tougher, I must be on my way to becoming a man. I'd read enough stories about boys and men and their dogs to know that if I wanted to be a man, I did need a dog. Not a cat, a dog. Real men didn't have cats—everyone knew that--and so soon I was petting every dog, mongrels especially or big purebreds, I could find in the village, on Garibaldi Square at the Saturday market, on the promenade at the water front, by the movie theater, at the castle—*everywhere*--all the while daydreaming of my own.

Without that thought—that you couldn't be a man without a dog--I'm sure I'd never have followed Ciccio to Magusa that night.

The dog in question was a white, mid-sized mongrel with a few large black spots, the kind of coloration dairy cows sometimes have, but he was no cow. He was skinny as a greyhound, and nervous as hell, and he appeared one day in our backyard, which angled from the back patio up into the olive groves. I heard a yelp and saw our maid, Elisa, with her one blue eye and one blind eye, trying to shoo him away. I said, "No, let him be," and she smiled the kind smile she always had for me, knowing how much I liked animals, and perhaps feeling, in her affection for me, that I deserved (for as long as my parents would let me keep it) a dog--even one as scrawny and mongrely as this one. "*Va bene*," she said. "*Vuoi dargli da mangiare? Would you like to feed it?*"

"Of course!"

I gave him a hotdog from the refrigerator--just the wiener – and when he had gobbled it up, another, and another.

"*Non troppo*," she said. "*Poverino, finirà per sentirsi male.*" *Poor little thing, it will get sick.*

"Yes," I said. Sometimes pity isn't a good thing, I remember thinking.

Elisa went about her business – laundry and mopping--and I sat on the flagstone stairs and petted the creature, whose coarse and dirty coat was a miracle to me. He was a *dog*, after all, and that's all that mattered. He had no collar. He might have been a runaway from one of the villages high in the hills. And he might soon be mine.

He sat beside me for a while, hoping I might give him more; and when I didn't, he began to wander off. I called. He stopped, looked at me, saw nothing in my hand, and kept on, disappearing into the grove next to us. I was disappointed, sure, but what could I do? Even if I petted him until my hand was numb, the dog would be thinking of food, worrying about it, and so would keep moving.

But the dog was back the next day, and around the same time. He had a cut over his right eye, and that worried me. He seemed healthy otherwise, though, and I wondered whether he was making the rounds – going from *villetta* to *villetta* on Via San Giuseppe, like a panhandler who knew who to hit up for money. Or had he come to our house – just ours--after rooting for food in the alleys down by the waterfront--because he remembered the wieners and the petting....and maybe even because he liked me.

I fed him for six straight days—wieners until they were gone, then old bread from the bakery near the school, then cans of cat food Nevis had never had a chance to eat, then leftovers from one dinner after another--and he returned each day in the afternoon as if he knew that on school days at least I wouldn't be home until then.

I was mustering the courage to ask my parents if I could keep him. We had no other pets; and though my mother talked constantly of getting a cat to replace "poor little Nevis," I knew it wasn't going to happen. My mother was afraid of things dying.

"Please," I rehearsed silently, "I've never had a dog before, and I'm old enough to take care of one, to be responsible for him….and I…*really really really want one!*" My speech needed work—especially the *really*'s—and I kept working on it.

On the seventh day, he didn't return. I'd been calling him Ciccio—a joke, since "Ciccio" means "chubby--and he had started on the fourth day to answer to his name. When he didn't appear on the seventh, I wandered around the olive groves near us, calling to him, but with no luck. Back at the house, I took cardboard from the trash, put two wieners on it, and laid them on the low wall in the backyard where the olive groves began, the ones that continued up the hill to Magusa and on to the old villas of the wealthy.

The next morning, the wieners were untouched, and I gave up rehearsing my speech. I knew what it meant. I was old enough to have heard that wandering dogs usually keep wandering, and that was better than thinking he'd been hurt, or worse.

Two days later--after a big test on Garibaldi's diary that I'd studied hard for with my friends--I was in the back yard moving the trashcans, and heard a yelp. It was from far away, up in the groves where the cobblestone path wound toward the hilltops, toward Magusa and Romito and the villas, so I thought nothing of it. A dog. Someone's dog. Not mine.

Then it yelped again, louder this time, and I went to the low wall to look over it. There, far up the hillside in the olive grove, was what certainly looked like Ciccio. He yelped again, started toward me in the grass and then stopped, as if someone had jerked him back. I blinked, trying to see. Was someone holding him on a leash? But I couldn't see any leash—I couldn't see anyone. Just grass, olive trees, and Ciccio.

He yelped again, tried to move toward me, and again something I couldn't see jerked him back. Was he tangled in something? Had he stepped in a trap of some kind?

I climbed over the wall and headed toward him. There was no tree near him. No rope, no net, no trap that I could see. His feet were free. What held him held him by the throat, jerking him again and again, but I couldn't see it.

Red doorways flashed before my mind's eye—even with my eyes open I could see them—and I felt a pull, the kind my friends had said they felt at the fork in the cobblestone path, the kind I'd never felt until now.

"Ciccio!" I called, feeling a chill on my skin despite the air's stillness, and walked faster. He whimpered and yelped in response, looking at me, trying to break away from what held him.

No matter how far and fast I walked up the hillside, through the trees, the distance between us somehow remained the same. It was like a dream where your feet don't work, where you want to run but can't. He would dig in his paws, struggling against the invisible leash, and I'd get maybe twenty feet closer; but then the invisible hand would pull at him again so hard he'd be wrenched around, fall, scramble up, and be dragged farther up the hill again toward....toward what pulled at me, too. *The path. The fork. The doorways.*

If you don't follow him, the breeze in the trees whispered, *whatever has him will have him forever.*

I was panting hard, walking as fast as I could, jogging when the hillside flattened even for a moment, but the invisible hand was even faster.

When he disappeared suddenly over a little rise, into tall grass, I was sure I had lost him; but as I came over the rise, stopping to catch my breath, there he was, sitting as dogs sit, panting too, happy to see me, his rump on the cobblestone fork.

And then he jerked, jerked again, and the invisible leash pulled him roughly once more toward Magusa.

The sun was beginning to fade. It was probably 6 o'clock now, and if I were to save him—though I had no idea how I would do that—it would have to be soon.

As the first houses of Magusa came into view, Ciccio did what I hoped he wouldn't. He was yanked suddenly to the side, left the path, fell, got up, and began half-running and half-falling again--but to where? How would I see him in the groves without light?

He had left the path just before the village began, and so I left it too, running now, dodging back and forth to make sure I could still see his whiteness among the trees, afraid that if I lost sight of him I would not, in the wind that had come up, hear his whine or yelps.

Why he was approaching the houses from the groves—why the invisible leash wanted this--I didn't know.

I expected to see at least a few lights from the houses, but there were none. In the growing shadows of the groves I hit my head on something, slowed, looked up, squinted, and saw around me what looked like bags, burlap bags, some large, some smaller, hanging from tree limbs. I didn't stop to inspect them— I'd lose Ciccio if I did--and if they were important, wouldn't my friends have mentioned them from their night in the groves? Maybe they held olive-picking tools? Maybe they contained food that was being aged, dried? It didn't matter. What mattered was that I kept my eyes on the flashes of white that were Ciccio.

Then I lost him again. It was near the back of one of the little houses, and all of a sudden his flashes were gone. My heart flipped and began to beat hard enough that I could hear it in my ears.

Then I heard a cough—yes, a cough—and I froze. When the

cough came again, I stepped behind a dark, gnarled trunk that couldn't possibly hide me if anyone really looked. I could see the back of the little house through the trees, in the deepening darkness, but I couldn't see who'd coughed. There was a wall the height of an ordinary man blocking any view of a backyard. A gate in that wall was open, but there was no one by it.

The cough came again, closer to the house, and I heard a door shut.

I stepped toward the gate, and, as I did, another bag hit me in the head. I looked up at it, but it was too dark to see clearly. I rubbed the side of my head, felt a wetness, but didn't bother looking at my hand in the dim light.

I reached the open gate in two or three strides, and there, sitting upright on the moss of a tiny walled-in yard, was Ciccio, staring straight ahead, perfectly still, making no sound.

I wanted to shout his name, but this was no place to make noise.

I took a step, expecting Ciccio to hear me, but he didn't move. He kept staring. It was as if he were deaf — and blind.

I was in plain sight now — he should have seen me — but he still didn't move.

I took another step, through the gate this time, and stopped breathing.

There, in the yard — two in one corner, one in the other — were three other dogs, a big black, hairy one, and two about Ciccio's size, just as mongrely.

They, too, were sitting and staring, motionless, silent.

Whatever holds them, I remember thinking, *is magic, and who am I to stop magic?*

There were four buckets of paint, too, I saw, in the middle of the mossy yard, and a stool beside them. Watching to make sure the other dogs didn't wake from their spells, I inched slowly into the yard. Whatever held the animals held them tightly.

Each bucket, I could see now, had a stick — just like the one in the bucket my friends and I had looked into that day in Magusa--and each bucket seemed to be full of paint, too.

And what else? I wondered. And then, as the wind picked up even more, I happened to look up at the one tree in the little yard. I don't know why I looked. There had been no sound. Nothing had moved in the tree. Perhaps I'd seen it—the bag hanging there--from the corner of my eye. Perhaps I'd even seen it dripping, like the bag that had touched my head. Whatever made me look, I squinted—

--and nearly screamed.

It wasn't a very large bag—much smaller than Ciccio--but a dog's head, its eyes closed, was sticking from the top of it, and there was something else—

I didn't want to see it, but I had to. I stepped toward the tree, squinted again and saw what was sticking from the bag just behind the head.

A dog's leg.

A leg that had been skinned.

What was dripping from the bag was blood—the dead dog's blood.

My heart thundered so loudly I couldn't think. Dog and leg and bag and blood floated in my head like snapshots, like a strange family album, and I thought I was going to faint. My hands shook, and my legs, which were cold now in my shorts, were shaking just as hard.

Can people hear it when we shake? my head asked stupidly.

Can people hear it when our hearts thunder?

I could, I knew, be killed as easily as the dog had been killed. It wouldn't even take magic to kill me. All it would take was a man or two and whatever weapons, whatever tools, they had— even bare hands. No one would hear me. Magusa was too far away. I needed to run—to get away from this place—and it didn't matter what direction I ran.

But I couldn't run—not without Ciccio.

I stepped over to him, and the instant I touched his head—I was afraid to, but more afraid not to—he looked up as if waking from a dream, whined, stood up, and began to move in little jerks, as if his legs weren't yet working.

I'd broken the spell—that was obvious. But if he yelped or whined, we might still be caught. I picked him up, hoping it would calm him, but it scared him, and he flopped and flailed in my arms. I lost my grip, he hit the ground, and all I could do was hold him by the skin of his neck, talking to him gently. "Don't make a sound, Ciccio. I'm here. *I'm here…*"

I heard the cough again inside the house, and then footsteps.

Ciccio whimpered once and the footsteps stopped, then got louder.

Telling Ciccio "Stay!", I ran to the two smaller dogs and touched them, ran to the big black dog to touch him as well, and, as their spells broke, too, the yard exploded in noise and motion—dogs running this way and that, the two smaller ones snapping at each other and the big black one woofing like a canon.

At that very moment a figure opened the back door and stepped out brandishing a big knife, one covered with something that glistened wetly.

The figure was small, but in the faint light that fell upon him he didn't look like any Southerner I'd ever seen. My father had taken us to Naples the summer before, and the summer before that we'd taken a cruise to Sicily and Libya; and this man looked nothing at all like the men I'd seen in those countries. He was squat, his head just as squat as his body, his ears like handles, his teeth too small for his mouth, and his face hairless.

I expected him to shout or scream, but, like the head that had appeared in the doorway that day with my friends, he made no sound. He moved, however, and it was toward me that he came.

The only thing that allowed Ciccio and me to escape was the two snarling little dogs and the big booming black dog, all of whom decided at the same moment to flee before the man could reach them. We all collided at the gate, but with a common mission—to get away from that knife—so no one snarled, no one bit, and in a moment Ciccio and I were out into the grove again.

It was dark and the bags, dozens of them, hung from the trees like terrible fruit. All I could do was run and try to duck them.

We had gone only a dozen yards when Ciccio stopped suddenly and began to back up. For a moment I imagined the invisible leash had gotten him again, but his legs were moving differently this time. He was whining, the way dogs do when they're afraid, and backing up. I squinted into the darkness and saw something move. In the corner of my eye, even closer to us, I saw something else move, too, and a bag in a tree started swaying.

There, straight ahead of us and touched by moonlight, was an upright figure taller than any man; and to our left, where the bag was swaying, another figure, tall enough that its head was in the tree branches. It was pushing at a bag with its snout, snuffling, sniffing.

Other than that, the two creatures made no sound, seemingly unaware of us, though that might change.

I could *smell* them. It had to be them. The smell of dogs, but not the kind you kept on your lap or let sleep on your bed--not Ciccio's kind of dog. It was the smell of a wild animal, wet, filthy, rancid from what it ate, a dog bigger than any dog, and upright—a creature from a dark dream.

I wanted to throw up. I wanted to scream. I wanted to lie down, cover my face, go to sleep and wake up from the nightmare of it; but Ciccio was whining next to me, backing up still, and I knew what we had to do, crazy as it was:

We had to return to the village.

Whatever was in the olive groves—and I didn't want to imagine what the faces of creatures as tall as olive branches, creatures that might sniff and swat at bags with dead dogs in them might look like--we were not going to get past them if we stayed in the grove; and frightening though the village was, it couldn't be any scarier than this.

Ciccio didn't need me to call his name. When I turned and began running, he was at my side.

I listened for heavy bodies behind us, heard nothing, but could not be sure. When they ran, did the creatures fall to four legs or did they run like men? Were their footsteps loud, or as quiet as wolves? We wouldn't be able to cut between the houses to reach the cobblestone path. The houses nearly touched. We would have to stay in the groves until we reached the path, and this we did, stumbling from the grass and trees onto the cobblestones and into the village at last.

I remember feeling grateful for the moonlight. Not much — a bright crescent moon, if any crescent moon could be called bright — but more light than there'd been in the groves behind the house.

Looking behind me for the creatures, I twisted my ankle on a cobble and fell. Ciccio waited for me to catch up; and when I reached him we both stopped for a moment to look up the path that ran between the houses--between the doorways with their paint and blood. *The blood of dogs.*

There was no one on the path except us, no doors started to open, no voices sounded in the houses.

And then I heard the baby cry.

I thought it was a whine from Ciccio, but the sound came again, and it was indeed a baby's cry.

There were no other voices. Just the baby's---as if there would never ever be anyone to pick it up and hold it.

As Ciccio and I stared at the empty path, we saw the creatures. We'd expected them from the groves behind us, but there they were, ahead of us somehow. I started to turn, ready to run once more, but these creatures too seemed not to see us. They'd been there on the path all along, I realized suddenly, but we just hadn't seen them. They'd been down on all fours, and now some of them were standing up.

They were looking at something on the path. The ones still on all fours were pawing at the cobbles. Those that had stood were staring and sniffing at the air.

Ciccio didn't move beside me. He didn't whimper, and for a

moment I was afraid the invisible leash had gotten him once more; but he was only hypnotized, just as I was, by the sight of the creatures, their big heads and chests, their long, sinewy legs, their fur—all of it lit faintly now by the crescent moon.

Was this how an ordinary dog--the kind that men knew and loved—acted when it felt true terror? Paralyzed? The sight and smell and soundless sounds of dogs so large that their jaws could snap you in half, and yet walking upright, like your master? Was this what ordinary dogs dreamed when they kicked in their sleep, whined, in the worst nightmares of their innocent, loyal lives?

Three of the creatures—there were six in all—were down on all fours, sniffing and pawing at the cobbles, while two remained upright looking at the same spot and a sixth sniffed at the nearest doorway, but didn't touch it. It sniffed the wood, the paint, jerked back again and again from what it smelled, and finally, as if tired of the impasse, returned to the five who were so intent on the stone path and whatever was there.

The baby continued to cry. The sound didn't come from a house, or the groves. It was as if the sound were coming from the ground, from the cobbles themselves.

I squinted, and, there, in the cobblestones at the creatures' feet, saw a faint light glowing.

How could light be coming from cobbles?

I took a step, then another, ready to run if the creatures turned to look at us. I managed four steps and squinted again. The light was indeed coming from the cobbles—as if through a crack in the pavement—and the creatures hadn't noticed us yet simply because they wanted so badly to get at that light.

The baby kept crying and the crying came from the light. How was it possible?

There was something—a room, space of some kind--under the cobblestone path, a place lit by a light, and in that space the baby cried. There was no other explanation. The creatures wanted the light because they wanted the baby.

They wanted the baby's blood.

I don't know how I knew this, but I did. It made sense of everything.

The creatures were going crazy. They were pawing frantically at the cobbles, at the light, at the sound coming from the light. They were smelling things I couldn't imagine, and the smells were driving them crazy. Two had broken away from the group and were sniffing at doors, daring to touch them now, pushing hard with their snouts, pawing with long paws, then jerking back as if the paint made them sick. *And why not?* I remember thinking. *Dog's blood. The wrong blood. The blood of kin.*

The baby had stopped, but was starting again.

And then one of the creatures saw us.

Perhaps it was Ciccio. Perhaps the creature smelled him, a brother. Perhaps it was my smell, or perhaps we'd made a sound. Perhaps, in its hysteria, it had looked everywhere and its eyes had finally fallen on us.

The creature stared at us, and as it did, its brethren turned in our direction, too, stood up, and cocked their heads. It was a dog they were seeing—a cousin, skinny and white with black spots--and that was all right--but there was something else standing by that dog, something upright and hairless and not unlike the baby that cried forever in the night.

They started toward us. I wanted Ciccio to run—to run to safety—"They don't want you!" I wanted to shout--but of course he didn't run. He started barking furiously and took a step toward them.

"No, Ciccio!" I grabbed him by the skin of the neck. He turned, snarled, stopped when he saw it was me, and let me pick him up, back legs kicking as if running for us both. Barely able to carry him, I stumbled toward the nearest doorway.

Whatever was inside the house would not, I told myself, be as bad as what was coming towards us. And there was no way I could outrun them whether they dropped to all four or stayed upright.

The door was unlocked, and I remember thinking giddily: *Why not?* The villagers knew the creatures couldn't enter. The crescent moon and cross and dog's blood would stop them, and the doorways were too small anyway for them to get through. The villagers knew this because it had all been happening for a long time, the squat smooth-skinned people and the dog creatures, the doorways and the crying baby. Perhaps at the beginning there had been no paint at all, just blood, old dark blood making the sign of the crescent moon and the cross. Perhaps (I thought giddily) the cross had been a--

I got us both inside and shut the door. Would there be a crash? Would the hinges hold? Would the creatures even try? Would there instead be a squat man in the darkness with a knife, a dog-skinning knife, who'd kill us both and put us in bags and hang us in the trees?

Nothing happened. There was no crash. No man in the dark came at us. There may have been sniffing and snuffling on the other side of the door, but how would I know, I was panting too loudly. I couldn't even tell if Ciccio was whining in my arms.

I blinked and saw a faint light near the floor. There was no light from another room. No light through windows, if there were any windows. Just that faint light near the floor.

I put Ciccio down, and he stayed.

When my eyes had adjusted as much as they were going to, I could see that the light was a crack in the floor, and, when I stepped over to it, that there was a handle on the floor, one dimly lit by that light.

There was a door in the floor — that's what it was--and the light was the same light that had been driving the creatures crazy outside.

I took the handle and started to pull up.

The baby was crying again. I could hear it now, and it wasn't coming from outside, from the path. It was coming, like the light itself, from below us, under the door in the floor. I started to pull again on the handle, and stopped. Why wasn't I afraid of what was below me, the light, the crying baby?

Because, a voice said, and it was my own, I know--the wisest one in me--*wherever the baby is, the creatures cannot be.*

The Bleeding Child

So I lifted the door in the floor and found the dirt and stone stairs I somehow knew would be there, ones lit faintly by the light somewhere beyond them.

Ciccio didn't want to go, and I pulled him onto the stairs with me, shutting the door over us quickly.

We followed both the baby's crying and the light, which grew brighter as we stepped from the last stone stair onto the bare earth, turned right into a passageway, and began to walk under what I knew was the front of the house, where the creatures no doubt still stood, trying to figure out how to reach the light that was driving them so crazy.

I don't know if I'm leaving things out when I say, as I always do, that we reached at last the big room, and the villagers there, and the baby in the center of them all. I have told this story — the story of Magusa — many times in my life, and, though I'm sure I have gotten some things wrong, I've remembered what matters most: The immense underground room, the villagers of Magusa filling it silently; the baby, on a stone table in the center, crying; hundreds of votive candles in the corners of the room to light it; lanterns on the dirt walls; and the light, though gentle and flickering, bright enough to shine through a crack in the cobblestone path above. Is all of this true? It must be since what we experience when we are young is burned like God's truth into our brains. What I saw that night — while my parents worried where I was — is as true as anything I have ever lived, and why I will tell this story again and again until my lips can no longer make words.

When Ciccio and I reached the great room--our noses full of dust, candle smoke, and something else — something metallic I'd smelled in the little yard where I'd saved Ciccio from the man's knife — the villagers were there, all of them, even the same squat man with the knife. And they were all there *because the baby was bleeding*.

They stood around it, watched it and did more than watch. But they were not what I was looking at. I was looking at the baby.

He was as dark-skinned as they were, but a baby like an other. He was naked on the stone table—an ancient, wor thing—and all I could think for a moment was how cold, ho incredibly cold, he must be. *To be alive, to be crying for someone hold you, and yet to lie on cold stone. What must it be like, my chil to do this forever?*

For he had indeed been doing it forever. This I knew, too.

And I recognized the metallic smell. The smell of copper. Th smell of blood. The baby was bleeding. He was bleeding slowl and he was bleeding a lot; but this was not why he was cryin He felt nothing as he bled. He was crying for his mother, wh wasn't there, and never would be, for she had died long ago.

The stone table under him, which was sloped, had littl channels, and it was down these channels that his blood, re and bright, like the paint on the doors, moved like honey int little cups—some stone, some ceramic, some metal—all old an chipped—as he cried and would not stop crying for someon who could not come. My brother, in the year of life he'd had had cried that way, too, but someone had always come.

Perhaps it was the way the villagers were standing, waitin patiently, or the way the baby lay on his back, arms and leg still, no one stepping to him, as if he, the baby, had the powe and they did not, that told me how long this had bee happening. Whether the blood happened only at crescer moons or at other times as well, it did not happen every nigh I knew. It had not happened the night my friends had staye the night in the trees, since they had met no dog-creatures.

To bleed forever....

He was bleeding from his hands and feet, from wounds he' been born with, and the villagers knew this, as their ancestor had known it, just as they knew that all they had to do to get th blood they needed in order to live forever, too, was wait for th right moon, and keep the creatures away, and let the bab bleed....

Born too soon, or too late, a voice said quietly, and whether was a voice from the room, the village, or my own mind makin sense of what should make no sense, I'll never know.

Born too soon, or too late, the voice said again, and it was true. *A mistake. An infant who would never take his true place in the world--even if he lived forever.*

There were four old women standing apart from the group, and it didn't take a genius to know who and what they were. They were the women who protected the village — and the baby--from the creatures who came every crescent moon, the creatures who wanted his blood, too, for what creature does not wish to live forever? They were the *streghe* who knew the spells that could drag dogs on invisible leashes to the village, who knew how to mix a paint that wasn't a paint, who knew the design a door should have, and how big the doorway should be. They hadn't invented this magic themselves. They had learned it from old women before them, and that was enough to keep their story going.

These are the women of the moon and blood, the voice said. *These are the women who protect a child who isn't theirs and give a village what it has needed for a thousand years.*

I wanted to go to the child, and I knew why. If I did, perhaps (a part of me whispered) I would find my baby brother there, pick him up and hold him, then take him home at last.

But he wasn't my brother — the idea was crazy--and the villagers would stop me anyway. They would have to. The squat man would produce his knife and that would be the end.

I hadn't made a sound, and neither had Ciccio; but a little girl turned at that moment and saw us. Her mother had given her a cup. The girl had drunken from it slowly, eyes closed, as if trying to taste what could not be tasted. And when she handed the cup back to her mother, she happened to look our way. She stared for a moment, tugged at her mother's black dress, and her mother turned too.

I'd imagined a shout would go up. I was sure one would. Ciccio and I had violated this room, discovered their secret, and a shout would go up. The villagers would swarm over us, and we would be beaten, perhaps killed — and why shouldn't we be? To intrude on their story. But a shout did not go up. A dozen faces were looking at us now, then another dozen, heads turning like echoes of a thought. But there were no shouts, no mutterings, and no knives.

They just stared--at the pale, red-haired boy and his skinny dog who were standing in the archway to the great room. They stared and blinked and I heard a great clock ticking somewhere. What I saw in their faces, their wide-set eyes that had seen the centuries pass and would see more, *world without end*, was not anger or insanity or fear.

It was a sadness, and, below that, a shame. I didn't understand it, and then did.

They had no choice. They had to drink his blood — the child's — to keep living, and because they did, they would never be free.

They too are forsaken.

So the villagers stared at the boy and his dog, both of whom were free to live, love and die, and, as they did, felt their prison even more, tasting it on their lips, on the rims of battered cups, in the coppery air, in the blood of a child that would cry for them forever.

Ciccio fidgeted beside me, and I fidgeted back. We were free to go, but where? The creatures were still out there on the path and in the groves, and would be there all night.

So I moved, Ciccio beside me, toward the flickering torches that led to the stairs and to the one-room house above them. No one followed. The villagers had turned away — only the little girl and two boys kept staring at us — and were again waiting for their cups to be filled. It would take all night, and it would take forever.

The stone floor of the house--the one with the door in its floor--was cold, but there was a blanket, one I found by crawling from corner to corner, touching everything I could until I found

66

it. It was wadded up in a corner and smelled of sweat, ordinary sweat, and something else — something strange--but I wasn't going to be picky. I wrapped myself in it and Ciccio lay down beside me. We would keep each other as warm as we could.

We woke twice to the sounds of footsteps near us. I expected bodies to lie down beside us or voices to tell us to leave, but neither happened. The footsteps stopped both times, and the room fell silent again.

Dawn light woke Ciccio first. There was one tiny window in the wall facing the groves, and dogs always wake before men. I woke a second later and looked around the room — at the little table and chairs I'd touched in the darkness, at the stone-and-mortar walls, and at the door to another room, one I hadn't known was there. I got up, folded the blanket, put it in a corner, and led Ciccio out, closing the door behind us quietly in case people were sleeping in that other room.

There was no one on the cobblestone path, but I could hear men talking in the groves beyond the houses. Olive-picking was what they did in the day, what they did with their lives that wasn't magic, and what they'd done in every country on this sea — this olive-growing sea--since the beginning. It was the one thing, the only thing, that let them live like ordinary men and women.

When I got home, my parents were relieved, but angry, too, as all parents are when their children scare them. I lied. I told them I'd hidden in an abandoned hut in the groves all night because three boys — ones who were probably drug users from Parma, in Reggio-Emilia--had chased me at sunset when I was looking for Ciccio, and how one even had a knife, and how I'd been too scared to leave the hut, fallen asleep and woken only at dawn. But at least I'd found Ciccio, see?

They believed me. What other story would make sense? I wasn't a bad boy. I didn't drink beer with friends (how could I?--my friends drank wine and only at meals), I didn't vandalize property, and no one my age in the village had a girlfriend.

My mother cried for a while, as if worrying about me had reminded her of my brother. My dad sighed—anger, as I've said, was never really his way—and kept patting me on the back in that gentle way of his. He'd grown up in Virginia, in a big family, and his own father, an educated man who loved books, had been soft-spoken too, though not as kind, I remembered.

My dad even patted Ciccio, to let me know, man to man, that everything was okay.

I didn't tell my friends what really happened. They'd have had question after question, and it would have taken days to explain, and maybe they'd have believed me, and maybe not. Mainly, they'd have been mad, feeling left out. Friends can be that way. "You almost got killed? How exciting! Why didn't you take us with you?"

I did worry about the child, but when, a few weeks later-- unable to keep quiet any longer--I started to tell my dad how I'd heard a baby crying in Magusa as if someone were hurting it, my dad said, "I'm not surprised, Brad, but there's nothing to do about it. Didn't your friends tell you? Magusa is empty. Everyone's gone. The olive trees in those groves have a blight, and the *carabinieri* think they've gone to the mountains to join the more radical communists around Montalcino. That certainly makes sense. I'm sorry about the baby. By the way, how did you hear it crying, Brad?"

I didn't answer, and he didn't press. He looked at me strangely for a few days, and then the conversation was forgotten.

My parents let me keep Ciccio, of course. He slept in my room after we bathed and de-flea-ed him. He chased lizards in the yard, but never, I was happy to see, caught them, and I threw a ball for him, which he lost interest in. I had him for a good week before he ran away. It wasn't any invisible leash that took him. He'd been acting stir-crazy, and the last time I saw him he was down by the wharf, letting a fisherman pet him. I called to him. He looked around, saw me, but didn't come; and he didn't return home that night either. *Wandering dogs usually keep wandering,* I remembered, and that was okay. It was okay, I told myself even then, to know love and magic — to have good friends or a scrawny dog or a terrible night in a village forgotten by God--for just a moment in time, and then to move on, living your life as you need to live it to become what you need to become, in a world where war sometimes does not feel like war at all, and blood does not have to mean dying.

VI

MARY

The American boy lived for a time in a village on the gentle Ligurian Sea. There he attended the same school as the village boys. His father was an officer in the military, assigned to a top-secret warfare center a few minutes to the north, but his mother, an educated woman who loved other cultures, did not want him to go to the base school to the south and hang around just American kids. She wanted him (she told everyone) to learn about the people there, to learn compassion. So the boy went to the school in the little fishing village, where he came to know the castle overlooking the cove, the witch with tuberculosis who lived in it, the fishermen who returned each afternoon with their lively catch, and the streets where the boy's schoolmates had been born and would, the boy suspected, always live. He came to know, too, out in the sunshine, the villas, some little, some large, on the hillsides, the olive groves where the boys played after school, where sharp-nosed witches tried to poison the cats, and where, when his friends went home for dinner, the boy could sit on a wall with the lizards and look down at the bay. There, the boy knew, a poet named Percy, had drowned in a storm a century and a half ago, and, a few years before that, his wife, the writer Mary Shelley, had perhaps dreamed the terrible dream that became her book, one the boy knew, about a monster made by a man.

Because the boy, too, felt he should write stories — felt it so much that he could not sleep at night--he found himself thinking of Mary Shelley and her husband when other boys would have absolutely no reason to.

The man who taught them French, Roman history, literature, geography, and most of their other subjects — everything except math, which was taught by a balding woman with a bad temper, and religion, which a big priest who rode a Vespa taught them — was a tall, thin man with curvature of the spine, and a lisp, named Brigola. The hunchback would stand before them in the cold room with its ancient furnace and, spittle gathering at the corner of his mouth, ask the boys politely to sit on their hands when he tested them orally. All of them except the

American boy knew the sign language every child in the village somehow managed to learn; and if their teacher did not make them sit on their hands, they would, when he wasn't looking, help each other with the answers. But if their teacher caught a boy signaling another, he would not scream at them; he would not shout. He would say simply, "You are a good friend, Paolo, but now is not the time."

Brigola knew by heart many long poems, both ones for study and ones for pleasure. He knew The Iliad and The Odyssey, or most of them anyway. "Cantami o diva del pellide Achille/L'ira funesta che infiniti addusse. Sing to me, o goddess!" He knew the epic poem about King Theodoric that began "Sul castello di Verona/Batte il sole a mezzogiorno," and ended with the old sad king taking a bath at the top of his castle. He knew French and English poetry, too, and he knew the Italian poems in English and French, as if he had translated them himself. There were some poems, because he never mentioned their authors' names, that the boys felt sure were his, though they kept it a secret. Poems about Mind's beauty, the wind, and birds in song – those subjects poets always wrote about. But abstract ones, too, ones that were difficult to understand. One about a tempest, and a silly one, the kind they themselves would write, about a cat. "Non piu! Non meno! Just a cat." Even when it wasn't literature they were studying, their teacher would stop, and, if it felt right (he would ask the boys' permission and they would of course give it) recite a poem, and the American boy would watch the man closely, trying to feel what the man was feeling, and be happy when he thought he did.

After school or on weekends during the summer, their teacher would sit fishing with a little pole on the wall of the promenade area by the wharf, where the main road passed closest to the little cove, and wait for the boys from his class, one or two a day, to find him. He never caught a fish. The American boy was sure of this. He was there simply so that the boys could find him. He wasn't married. He loved a woman, people said, in the next cove – a woman named Amelia – but he never saw her. She could not love a hunchback, people said, and she had told him so. He had no children and his parents had passed away, so he had lots of time to sit on the wall with his pole and wait for any boy who wished to talk.

Mary

The American boy watched all of this and wanted to go to him, but found it difficult. The boy would stand outside the bakery or the beach-goods store and, if their teacher were there on the wall, there would be a different boy each time. Brigola would be holding his pole and the boy might be holding one, too--or not. What did they talk about? the American boy wondered. What do you talk about with your teacher when the pig production of Calabria or the length of the Po River isn't really that important and you're sitting with him looking out at a bay where a famous poet drowned a long time ago and his wife dreamed a dream that became a famous book?

The boy was writing a story. He was, in fact, writing it in class — one about a dream he had, about snakes swarming over the nearby hills, one that had come true--when he should have been paying attention to their teacher, who was talking about Garibaldi's "March from Quarto to the Volturno." The hunchback stopped the class and said, "What are you writing, ragazzo?" Face hot, the boy held his breath, and, deciding to be honest, answered: "I am writing un racconto, un racconto di fantasia. A fantasy…." The hunchback looked at him, and a miracle happened. The man smiled. He did not get angry the way the boy's mother might have, nor did he have contempt in his eyes, as many teachers might. Instead, Brigola continued to smile until at last he said: "I wish you the best of luck with your stories, ragazzo. As you know, the great author Mary Wollstonecraft Shelley lived here for a while, sometimes happy, sometimes not. She had many dreams, and her husband drowned not far from here. Lerici was an unhappy place for her, and finally she left it…." Their teacher blinked, as if distracted, and then added: "If you publish your stories some day, Bradley, please send them to us." There was no sarcasm. The man was sincere. But how did he know the boy was writing stories — more than this one? Gianluca, his best friend, was the only one who knew. Had he sat on the wall one day after school and told their teacher?

"I will," the boy said. But he did not write in class the rest of the week. When he started writing again, it was a story about a man, a hunchback, who loved beauty so much that he grew weak and died. He didn't write much in class that week, just enough each time that the *story could move forward, that the people in it could do what they needed to do, and he knew their teacher was watching him as he did...*

VII

THE WOMAN WHO WAITED FOREVER

The military, like every other world, has its social classes, with a sometimes-impossible chasm between officer and enlisted — something that even a foxhole or military hospital has a hard time breaking down, and something that will always be haunted by the dead whispering of injustice. When you're the son of a Naval Academy graduate, you know that those crewcut, knockdown, book-avoiding kids on the school bus with you in the sunny port of San Diego are going to play rough touch football with their dads while you play a dignified game of tennis with yours, that their families will ride muscular power boats on the bay while yours prefers the grace of sailboats, and that yours will belong to a sedate yacht club while theirs will throw wonderful, rowdy barbecues on public beaches. Those kids wouldn't be caught dead doing what you're asked to do at the parties your father and mother have for the other officer families, namely, helping serve hors d'oeuvres in little mahogany bowls. In fact, they'd probably pants you if they caught you doing it. All because they're the sons of the enlisted, while you're the son of a three-striper.

You may envy them their confidence and scars, the colorfulness of their lives, but even at your age you know that family is destiny. The privileged, though cursed by their own ghosts, are still privileged, wouldn't have it any other way, and haven't since the beginning of time, whether in war or peace.

So it was a shock, especially to the adults, to encounter--at my father's submarine warfare center--an officer's family that didn't behave like one at all, that acted "enlisted" in the very worst sense of the word, and that, because it did, threatened the cosmological order of things in the tiny community of officer families there. The two sons, Keith and Bobby, could certainly have held their own with the toughest, roughest enlisted Army, Navy and Marine kids on that school bus in San Diego. And the

daughter—well, the daughter could have held her own, too, bu
in other ways.

Their father was a commander, too, like mine--Commande
John Speer--and there were strange things about the famil
beyond the fact that his two sons, Keith, at 13, and Bobby, at 1!
were tough as nails, boasting, in fact, as one of their favorit
pastimes, shooting lit cigarettes out of each other's mouths witl
a 22. Their sister—whose name, Chastity, said it all—was
model United Nations, that is, she had the hots for any boy c
any nationality she could find; and find them she did a
Lungamara, the swimming cove where the families of officer
from Italy, America, Germany and France—those who worke
at the NATO Center thirty minutes north in the industrial por
of La Spezia—could sun themselves on the weekends and swin
in the crystal-clear waters of the Ligurian Sea. Chastity was, w
were convinced, "sexually active," though the term we all use
was the much less clinical "slut." To the adults, Chastity'
mother was one too, but for the strangest reason: She wa
pregnant at 42. Her husband was the father of the baby, o
course; but in those days, you just didn't have a kid at 42 with
13-year difference between your youngest kids. It was a scanda
in the officer community.

The Speer boys were being educated at a monastery nea
Rome; so I didn't meet them for a while, and they weren'
around much; but when they were, I was supposed to play witl
them because they were officer's kids, too, but also because m
parents didn't know what troublemakers they were. I wondere
if the monks beat them. I couldn't imagine them obeying fat littl
men in brown robes. I couldn't imagine them obeying thei
father either, but for all I knew he was even tougher than the
were.

Why I played with them, scary as they were, I don't know.
didn't have a dog anymore, and I wasn't going to go to th
mountains looking for the Magusans or any other strang
villagers simply for the excitement of it. But I did wan
excitement—I was a teenager, after all--and my friends fron

school were, I'd begun too think, a little too nice to provide it. The Speers had that weird charisma all bad boys have for boys who are a little too "good." They're the stuff of our secret fantasies: "If I had the courage—and wouldn't get in trouble—that's what I'd do too--shoot cigarettes out of someone's mouth with a gun!"

"Speer? What nationality is that?" I asked Keith one day as we headed down from my family's *villetta*, our little house, to the next cove, his brother somewhere else for a change.

"What do you mean—nationality? We're Americans, asshole."

He'd call you every name in the book, but he'd still hang out with you. Whether he really liked you, you never knew; but he'd appear and want to hang out because you were the only thing available.

"I know that, Keith. I mean, your people—your ancestors—what country did they come from?"

He was a staring at me as if I was accusing him of something.

"*My* people are from Scotland," I said stupidly, trying to make the sparks leave the air. "But that was a couple hundred years ago."

"Well, la-di-da, Brad."

We walked on for a while. Why was he so upset?

"It's a German name," he said at last, "but that doesn't mean we're Nazis."

"I wasn't saying you were a Nazi." I wanted to laugh, but this was a serious matter for him. I wanted to say, "Nobody's a Nazi now, Keith--World War II was a long time ago," but didn't.

"Gee, thanks."

"Why...why would anyone think you're a Nazi?"

"Because of the name."

"I didn't even know it was German."

We kept walking and, just as I'd given up on an answer, Keith said:

"If you know history, my dad says, you know the name Speer."

"He was a Nazi?"

"Of course."

"Why does that make *you* a Nazi?"

"Jesus, Brad," he said. "You're dense."

I was silent.

"Because you're related?" I said at last. "You're the same Speer he was?"

"Shit, yes. Distant cousins...."

I didn't say anything after that. It had been fifteen years since the war had ended, and here was a kid my own age who was still living it. The Speer kids were as American as you could get—nothing German about them, let alone Nazi—and here was Keith afraid of what someone would think.

The Speer boys left on Sunday to return to their monastery, and I went back to playing with my friends from school—Carlo, Maurizio and Gianluca—boys I felt I understood better than I understood Keith. Fantasies aside, Keith made no sense to me— shooting a 22 at his brother's face, ringing doorbells and running, stealing things for no reason, talking about girls in the grossest ways, being the worst possible ambassador from America, and feeling much more uneasy about an old war than my village friends did, though they had relatives who'd lost arms and legs and eyes in that war and many of their aunts wore black because they'd lost their husbands in the war.

Later, the next year, I'd be playing in the olive groves below our house with those friends and a fourth, Armando Suraro, whose mother was German who spoke with a German r, and two other boys we didn't really know. One of those boys, frustrated at losing a game, would get mad at Armando and call him a "Nazi." Armando would cry. He would cry hard. But that day hadn't happened yet. The events at the long-abandoned German hospital in the next cove hadn't happened either, so I hadn't yet learned that an old war could reach beyond death to children born after its official end.

And I hadn't yet learned the faces that magic could wear. The next time I saw Keith, Bobby was with him. Their dad had bought them bows and arrows, and they wanted to go shoot them somewhere. I liked the idea, too. Anything—even boring paper targets on trees—was better than shooting the lizards of the groves with blowguns, which some of my friends still did. Since my parents didn't know about the 22 and cigarettes—or the doorbell ringing—my dad, who was a good guy, said, "Sure, Brad, you can have a bow and arrows, too. Where are you going to shoot?"

"Keith wants to go to the cove between here and San Terenzo."

Had I known what was going to happen, I'd have said instead, "The cove with the old German hospital," knowing my father would have said "no."

"Okay. But I want you and Keith--and anyone else who's going--to check in beforehand."

When we were ready, there were four of us. Keith, me, a friend of Keith's from the monastery school, and an Italian kid I'd just gotten to know. His name was Marco, and he was from Vecchia Lerici, the old part of the fishing village, the alleys of fishermen and seamstresses—in other words, working class. How I knew him when I was in the *scuola media*—with the sons of "professionals," the middle and upper classes—and not the *scuola tecnica*, where he was, where the blue-collar kids went after they graduated from elementary school, was a simple story. I'd always liked fishing—you sometimes do when you're a Navy brat—so I often fished on the wharf or on the rocks by the *passeggio*, that waterfront walkway where young couples appeared at sunset and strolled peacefully while old people sat on the benches and enjoyed watching them. Sometimes our teacher would fish there too, so we'd fish together, though he never caught anything and I didn't do much better. Even at my age I knew—we all did--that he sat there on the rocks so that his students could talk to him if they wanted to. He didn't do it for himself, in other words; he didn't do it because he was lonely. Rumor was that he loved a woman in San Terenzo, one he had met during the war, and that she had either died in that war or would not marry him because he was deformed; and that, either way, he could not have her. So he must have longed for love, but that didn't mean he was lonely. He'd been born a hunchback and it had only gotten worse. The villagers liked him, admired him, and felt from him the same soul we all felt; and, though he had to return each night to his apartment, where he lived alone, he didn't feel sorry for himself. He wasn't like that. He loved his students, and he wanted to be there for them whether in school or out.

One day after school I was sitting with him, and we were fishing, but not really. We weren't even talking. We were just sitting there, and a boy—my age, but smaller--walked over to us and sat down too with his pole. He nodded, but said nothing, and our teacher said, "*Buon giorno, ragazzo,*" and the boy nodded again. "*Buon giorno, signore,*" he answered. There was only one hunchback in the village, our teacher, so the boy knew who he was.

He wasn't a shy boy. He was simply quiet, in the same way that the fishermen of the village were quiet. In Naples and elsewhere to the south, I'm sure fishermen sang. Maybe on Sardinia they sang, too, but in this village the fishermen, whether on the wharf dumping their catch onto the tables where the fisherwomen could sell them, or on their boats getting things ready for their next trip, or putting the nets away for the day, they were silent. There was a rhythm to what they did—I could feel it—anyone could—and perhaps, I often told myself, this was their singing.

"What fish are you angling for?" our teacher asked the boy. I'm not sure the boy even had bait, but our teacher was not going to embarrass him.

"Anything."

"For 'anything'," our teacher said, with that lisp that softened everything, "you should try as many kinds of bait as possible. Would you like to try what I have?"

The boy nodded, and our teacher handed him a little bucket of bait—cheese, tiny bread balls and earthworms--reaching behind me stiffly to give it to him since I was between them.

"Thank you," the boy said.

We caught nothing, but were happy enough. The afternoon sun caught the waves by the little jetty, but did not blind us when we looked. The brightly colored fishing boats — the ones that had left before dawn and come back in at noon — bobbed in the cove; and the castle, the one that Pisa and Genoa had fought over for centuries, looked down at us. I wondered if the unhappy witch who lived there, spitting at the tourists, could see us and was giving us the evil eye, *mal'occhio*; but in the late afternoon sun, sitting with two people who seemed to enjoy sitting with me, I didn't really care, and the question wriggled away like a minnow in the waters below us.

"This time of day," our teacher said, "isn't the best time to catch fish, of course."

The boy said nothing.

"But it is nice to sit here."

The boy gave a little grunt.

It felt as if our teacher were waiting for something, though I had no idea what. It wasn't fish. Even when he got a nibble, he seemed shocked that there should be something out there in the water. "What in God's name is *that*?" he would say.

He was waiting for something, but what? For the boy to talk? That wasn't like him either, to care whether a boy spoke or not during fishing. Silence didn't bother our teacher. Little did. Even when boys were bad in class — using the sign-language that everyone somehow knew to help each other answer oral-exam questions — he usually laughed or said something kind.

"May we know your name?" our teacher asked.

The boy looked at me, then at him, then at me again, and said, "Marco."

"Well, Marco, it has been pleasant sitting with you and Brad this afternoon, but I must now go home to grade dictation papers. I hope you and Brad will use the bait bucket. You may keep it, in fact, if you would like. I have many others."

What he'd been waiting for, I knew then, was the right

moment to leave — the right moment to ask Marco's name, and then to leave us, but in a way that would make us stay and fish together and perhaps talk--an American boy from an officer's family and a Ligurian boy from the dark, old part of town, the kind of kid I didn't know, but should, just as he should know someone like me, but would not if our teacher did not handle his departure perfectly and leave us to become friends for at least an afternoon.

I also knew that our teacher did not have other buckets, that he valued, old and battered as it was, this bucket; but that if he left it with us, we would have to stay.

Marco and I used up the bait. He caught two *bocca d'oro's*, and I caught a *sparo*--all three of them little fish, but pretty enough, shining in the late afternoon light. At least we'd caught something--which does matter to boys even if doesn't matter to their teacher.

When the bait was gone — our fish dangling from strings in our hands — Marco tried to give me the bucket.

"No, you should keep it." I started to add, "I already have one," but I knew how that might, if he were sensitive, sound: *I, the middle school kid, have more than you.* Instead I said: "You heard him say it. He wants you to have it."

Marco nodded, and that was that. We were friends, as our teacher had planned.

The day Keith and his friend from the monastery school--another American, but a civilian--appeared at our house with their bows and arrows--and I had mine, bought the day before at our monthly trip to the PX in Livorno — Marco appeared suddenly at our *villetta's* door, too, fishing pole in hand.

"Will you be fishing today?" he asked me in Italian.

"No," I answered. "I'm going with an American friend to shoot bows and arrows."

Keith and his friend had walked over and were standing beside me. Keith didn't like it when I spoke Italian, and he was staring at Marco. We were about to go in to see my father — to hear his "rules" before we headed to the cove--and Keith, annoyed that we might get a long lecture, wanted to get going.

"Marco," I said in Italian, "this is my American friend, Keith." Keith's Italian was terrible, and so was Bobby's. For some reason the monks weren't making them learn it — or maybe they were trying and the Speer boys were refusing.

Keith scowled and said, "His name's Marco?"

"Yes."

"So, Marco...." Keith said to him in English, not at all friendly, and for a moment Keith and Marco stared at each other. Keith obviously didn't want Marco around. We were getting ready for an adventure, Keith was in charge, and he didn't want someone who could speak only Italian tagging along.

But when I looked at Marco's face, I saw no hostility — the kind Keith's eyes had. I saw simply a look that said Marco recognized the kind of boy Keith was; that boys like Keith were much more common in Marco's world than in mine; and that if this was the kind of boy Keith — my American friend — was, so be it. The world was what it was, and when you were from Vecchia Lerici, you accepted it.

"*Vuoi venire con noi? Ho due archi e molte frecce,*" I said to Marco. *Do you want to come with us? I've got two bows and extra arrows.* Had Keith been able to understand it, it would have made him mad; but I said it.

"*Come no!*" Marco answered—"Of course!"--and this surprised me, though it shouldn't have. He might have to accept that the world was full of boys like Keith, but that didn't mean he had to be intimidated.

"He's coming with us," I said in English.

"No way!" Keith said.

"You've got a friend. Marco's mine."

"Where did you find him? He looks Sicilian."

"We went fishing with our teacher." That was a lie. It implied that Marco was in my class at school, and that he was not, as

Keith would put it, a "peasant." But I wasn't going to give Keith what he wanted.

"Why would you go fishing with your teacher? He's got a lisp. What a fag."

I didn't say anything. I knew that arguing with Keith was hopeless, and that if Keith got angry and loud enough, my dad might appear and tell us we couldn't go.

I just stood there waiting, thinking about our teacher and how he waited, too, not trying to push things into happening.

"Ah, hell. He can come if you want him to, but he'd better not fuck things up."

I gave Marco one of my bows and a quiver of arrows—all new—and the four of us went in to see my father in the living room.

"Who's this?" my dad asked.

"Marco, a friend from the village."

"Well… Please tell Marco that I don't know enough Italian to say what I'm about to say in Italian, but that you can translate, Brad."

When I'd told Marco, my father looked at all of us, took a breath, and began:

"Boys, you can go to that cove, but you've got to follow these rules. If you don't and I find out later, you'll all be grounded. Keith's dad will back me up on this, I'm sure."

We waited. Keith looked ready to blow, so we were looking at him as much as we were my father.

"Find a place that's safe for shooting. Make sure there's a hill or cliff behind it so your arrows stop there. Make a line—a line you'll all shoot from—and no shooting if anyone's over that line, if anyone's between you and the targets. You've got paper targets, right? No one shoots if anyone's walking toward the targets, checking them, changing them. And no shooting at anything other than the targets—I don't care how tempting a tree or a shack or a wagon looks. Got it?"

We all nodded, even Keith, even Marco, who hadn't understood a word.

"Got it," I said.

Outside, Keith said, "Yeah, right. Your dad's as candy-assed 'strack' as mine is. How do you stand him?"

I didn't answer. I knew we weren't going to do everything my dad had said—some of the rules were silly—but I liked my dad, even if I wasn't going to say so.

On the path to the cove, I tried to translate for Marco what my father had said. Marco's eyes rolled at one point when he realized how many rules there were, but he listened, helped me with some of the words, and nodded in that quiet way of his.

It took us no time at all to get there because it was downhill most of the way. About halfway—among the *villettas* where Keith and his brother had rung the doorbells so much they barely worked anymore—Keith's brother caught up with us, panting, bow and arrows in his hand, too. I'd never really seen him this close up. He had better things to do usually than hang out with us. He was tall, like his father, and thin and quiet, not at all as loud as Keith, and calmer, more confident--his eyes calculating, aware of everything around him. He had a small scar over his left eye, and a long scar on the back of his hand. Had he gotten them in fights, by rough-housing with Keith, or— at least the one over his eye—from a bad 22 aim?

Why he wanted to hang out with us that day, I had no idea, but he obviously wasn't embarrassed that he had a kid's bow in his hand. His was bigger than ours and the feathers on the arrows weren't so colorful, but it was still a kid's.

He was squinting down the path toward the cove, trying to see something, and we let him lead. Keith tried to stay alongside him, but before long was walking with us.

When we reached the bottom of the hill, where the cove started, the houses disappeared and the cobblestone path became dirt. Bobby was craning his neck looking for something not in the cove, but up between the hills. He said, "There's an old hospital up there. I want to see it."

None of us answered. Not even Keith.

I'd seen the hospital before, I realized—at a distance anyway—but had forgotten it was in that cove. My father--as we'd driven to La Spezia one Saturday for a tennis party for the officers' families--had turned off the coast road and onto a gravel one that led up between the hills--"Just out of curiosity," he'd said. He loved taking side roads, and my mother never minded. We had time.

The gravel road had stopped at a little garden with a marble statue of a woman, and from there forked in two directions—one north to what looked like a big villa in the hills and the other south to a large building of some kind, much closer and down on the flat. You could see the building from where we sat in the car, and it looked old and abandoned.

"Who does this land belong to?" my mother asked. She'd probably ask the *Contessa* Musetti, too, the next time they had tea at the Villa Musetti; but maybe my dad knew.

"Don't know," he said. "That building is an old German hospital. Who owns it now, though, I have no idea."

We turned the car around, and, as we left, I glanced back at the statue. It was a naked woman—a beautiful woman, too--so of course I was interested. She didn't look Greek or Roman; she looked more modern, "Romantic," as our teacher would say. Her hips weren't as big as a classic statue's, and her thighs were thinner, her arms long and beautiful. This was all very exciting, of course—I was 13 and statues like her were exciting—but both the lizard that sat on her head, doing little push-ups, and the sad and wistful look on her face killed it. Was she from a legend or myth, or was she someone who'd actually lived, someone long dead now? And why was she sad? Why would you want a sad woman greeting everyone on the road to your nice villa?

There wasn't really any way to cut directly from the dirt path through the olive groves to the hospital. There were old walls—some as old as the Etruscans, people said—littering the orchards, and it was a pain in the ass climbing over them. So, after a couple of minutes of trying, we returned to the dirt path and just walked until we found the gravel road, took it, and finally reached the little garden and the statue.

I stood staring at her. Her head was gone.

"You like tits, Brad? She's got nice ones." It was Keith, of course. "Hey, someone took her head!" He laughed and his brother laughed too. Then they looked at each other, and I knew they'd been here before.

Someone had indeed taken her head away. It wasn't lying around anywhere that we could see. Why anyone would want the sad-faced head of a statue, I didn't know.

Bobby was walking up the fork toward the hospital, so we followed. I looked up once at the villa on the hill, but it was so far away—as if the hospital and it couldn't possibly be related— that I didn't really worry about anyone watching us. Without binoculars they wouldn't be able to see us.

When we reached it, the building was even bigger than it looked from the garden. It was wood and corrugated metal, big and tall, with lots of windows around the top of it to let light in. It didn't look like a hospital. Why build one this way—just one floor, all those windows? Maybe it hadn't been a hospital originally. Buildings got appropriated during war. I knew that.

It was big and quiet and no one else was there. Birds whistled in the groves on either side of it. The sounds of the cars on the coastal road didn't reach this far. It was peaceful.

Bobby was already at the front door, which was unlocked, a big chain dangling from it, the lock that once held it in place long gone.

"I can't believe no one's ever been here," Keith announced. He meant kids—kids like us, or him and his brother. No one had used spray paint on the outside walls. No one had broken the high windows with rocks.

Bobby didn't answer. As if on a mission, he'd pulled the chain aside, opened the door, and stepped inside. We followed.

What I saw inside made no sense for a moment, and then it did. I'd been right. There was only one floor. The high windows let the light in, and it fell on a dusty, littered pavement. It had been a factory of some kind, but the machinery had been removed during the war. Cots must have covered the floor when it was a hospital, hundreds of them, with partitions that were no longer there, and tables for medical supplies and equipment, whatever hospitals had back then. Other than medicine and gauze and splints and surgery, what could you give wounded soldiers that might help them heal? You could give them sunlight--and the windows did that. Was it a cold building, though? It had to be, all that glass and the high ceiling; and you'd need blankets, lots of them.

Bobby was kicking at something, a piece of wood. There were no signs that anyone — beggars, gypsies from the south — had been here in recent times, lighting fires on the floor to stay warm or cook with.

The light from the high windows reached most of the floor, but in the four corners there were shadows.

Something made a noise, a tiny noise, in the corner nearest us, and we turned, waiting to hear it again.

"Rat?" I said.

"Who cares?" Keith said--as if this, like everything, were a test of his courage.

The sound came again, but not from the same corner. A creaking this time. The floor was cement. Only the building itself was wood. Why wouldn't an old wood building creak?

"More than one," Bobby said, snorting.

Keith went to the corner nearest us, kicked the litter around to show off, jumped when the creak came again — this time from the great beams near the ceiling--and walked back looking as nonchalant as he could.

"Scared now?" Bobby said to him.

"Fuck you," Keith answered.

"Fuck you too, dipshit." Bobby was laughing. Nothing scared him; that was obvious.

"Isn't that a table?" I asked. I could see a table in the shadows of the corner where Keith had kicked at things — the corner where the first sound had come from.

"Who gives a shit?" Keith said. "This is boring. Let's go back and knock that statue over."

"Can't," his brother said, looking up at the windows now. "It's bolted down."

So they'd tried. Were they the ones who'd taken the head?

This embarrassed Keith, and when Keith felt embarrassed, he got angry.

"What are you looking at?" he said to Marco, who was looking at both of them. Keith's friend was looking at them, too, but Marco was the annoyance — the one who shouldn't be along because I, not Keith, had asked him.

Marco didn't need to understand Keith's words. He knew the tone. He knew it better than I did. He simply shrugged.

"Nothing in here." Bobby was heading for the door. Keith followed, and in a moment, relieved, so did the rest of us.

We found Bobby standing on the side of a little hill beside the building, still looking up at the windows. "They're perfect," he said, and they were. Not one of them was broken — on this side of the hospital anyway. But that's not what he meant.

He notched an arrow — he seemed to know what he was doing — took a breath, and let it fly.

The arrow didn't shatter the window. It didn't bounce off it. It went through it like a bullet, making a hole about the size of your fist. I felt it go through. We all did. *A perfect hole in perfect glass.* This was even better — more exciting — than if the window had just broken. You couldn't do that with a rock. This was precision. We stared, amazed.

"All right!" Keith shouted.

"Beautiful," his brother whispered.

Then the guilt hit. This was *not* what I thought we were going to do today. It certainly wasn't what my dad thought we were going to do. And it was not what we *should* be doing. Trees or bushes or bottles or a shack or an ox cart — that was one thing, but this....an old building someone owned, perfect windows, ones we were breaking. I could hear my parents discussing it--

trust, betrayal, "he's not the son we thought he was." *Vandalism*—which meant destroying something you didn't care about but that someone else did.

Not to be bested by his brother, Keith had notched an arrow, too, even as Bobby notched his second, and was letting it fly.

Neither Keith's friend nor Marco nor I were notching arrows. Not yet.

"I don't think...." I started to say. "My dad—"

"Oh, for Christ's sake," Keith said. "Why did you even come, Brad?"

That was the most shaming thing he could have said, and it worked. It meant: "You'll never have the courage. You'll never be a real man." Keith was a master at shame.

"I don't think—" I started again.

"No one cares what you think," he said.

"It's an abandoned hospital," Bobby was saying, not looking at me, though meaning it for me.

He was right. It was abandoned, and abandonment meant that no one cared—no one cared enough about it to keep it up. How could this be vandalism if no one cared? It wasn't as if we were going to set fire to the place. If Keith or Bobby started to do that, I'd run. I'd shout "No!" I'd take Marco with me and we'd run. I wouldn't be a part of *that*, and because I knew I wouldn't—I swore I wouldn't--

--it was easier to notch the first arrow.

And because I notched mine, Keith's friend and Marco notched theirs.

We all let fly. We were following one of my dad's rules at least. We were standing on a hillside, in a line, and the windows were so high no one could possibly get shot. Wasn't that—safety--more important than the windows?

Keith and Bobby had more arrows than we did, so when we ran out, we just stood there watching them. Most arrows had hit windows, and we'd all tried to make sure—for the *perfection* of it—that each window had only one hole in it.

"Well, go get your arrows," Keith said smugly.

"Not if you're going to keep shooting."

"We're not going to keep shooting," he said. "You think we're stupid?"

I wanted to say, "No, but I don't trust you," but didn't.

"They're your arrows, too," I said instead. "Why don't you and Bobby come?"

"Because we don't need them yet."

Bobby wasn't saying a thing. He was looking at the windows, as if counting.

"Okay," I said instead, "but don't shoot."

"Jesus, what a wimp."

Bobby laughed at that, but was still counting. I looked at the windows. There were only two that didn't have holes in them. When we got back to the hillside, Bobby was going to take those two windows himself, I knew. Our shooting was over, and so was Keith's. We could always go to the other side of the building, but on that side we might be seen from the villa. We were done--unless of course Bobby said, "Screw perfection. Let's hit those windows with everything we have," and the one-hole-per-window rule no longer mattered. But I didn't think he would. He liked the perfection too much.

I started down the hillside to the building's front door, Marco and Keith's friend behind me.

Inside, arrows were scattered everywhere, and we started picking them up. Before we left the house, we'd all marked our arrows so we'd know who they belonged to—so that was no problem--but it was going to take awhile to find them all on a floor this big, littered as it was with wood, corrugated metal and other junk. Keith and Bobby would have to wait. We were the ones doing the work.

Just as Marco—who was standing about twenty feet away from me—picked up an arrow, looked at it, and said, "*Di chi sono le frecce con le croci?*" *Who do the arrows with crosses on them belong to?*—a window above us, one of the two that were still intact, cracked; and the arrow that passed through it arced slowly through the air, down through the sunlight, hitting

Marco in the neck, near his shoulder.

Marco screamed. I may have screamed too. I don't remember. All I remember is Marco—pale, eyes frantic, hands shaking--grabbing at the shaft, wanting to pull it out, but not wanting to because when he touched it, it hurt too much. Keith's friend ran over and we both stood beside Marco. There wasn't much blood, but there was this arrow sticking out of him, and we didn't know what to do. We'd seen lots of westerns, but we still didn't. Did you try to pull it out? It didn't have an arrowhead on it. It was just a wooden arrow with a smooth metal tip on it. Could you pull it out safely? Were you supposed to wait and let a doctor do it? How could you pull it out safely if the person was trembling and might at any moment start screaming and flailing at you?

"Stop moving!" I said.

"*Che dolore! Che dolore!*" Marco was saying, but he wasn't crying. He was being strong.

"I know it hurts, Marco, but you've got to stop moving. It's in your neck." We could hear shouting outside on the hill. Keith and Bobby had heard Marco's scream and knew why he was screaming.

They were inside in no time, running toward us, Keith without his bow, his brother still holding his. I jumped to conclusions.

"You shot him, you asshole!" I screamed at Bobby, not caring if it made him mad. "Keith said you wouldn't keep shooting and you did."

Bobby was looking at the arrow, at Marco's neck, Marco's face, how hard he was shaking. He took Marco by the arm and said, "We need to get him out of here."

"You shot him," I shouted again.

"No, I didn't," Bobby said. He didn't say it angrily. He just said it, as a fact, looking at Keith.

Then I knew what had happened. There had been only those two windows left. Keith had known his brother wanted them. Not to be bested, Keith had gone for one of them. Even though we were inside, he'd gone for it, thinking, "What's one arrow in such a big building and only three boys?" He hadn't thought it would hurt anyone; but when he'd heard the scream, he'd dropped the guilty weapon.

"You said you wouldn't shoot," I said to Keith hoarsely. It was stupid to keep saying it, but I didn't know what else to say.

"Fuck you," Keith said back, and I thought he was going to hit me. What else could he do, given what he'd done?

"We need to get him out of here," Bobby said again, his hand on Marco's good arm as he tried to guide him toward the door. "Tell him to stop wiggling, Brad. Tell him it's dangerous."

"I already did," I said, but did it again.

Marco did his best to stop wiggling, to not grab at the arrow again, and we were all heading toward the door--

When a figure, a woman, stepped from the shadows of the corner.

We stopped dead. Were we imagining this? No, it was definitely a woman, a young woman, and she was looking at us silently. Where had she come from? Was she the one who'd made the first sound, and had been watching us all this time? But Keith had checked that corner, hadn't he? He'd kicked litter around there, hadn't he? He'd have seen her. There'd been a table in that corner, nothing more, right? Or had he missed her in the shadows? Had she been sitting on the floor maybe, and he'd missed her? Why would anyone do that, though? Why would anyone, especially a woman, sit in the shadows of this building watching us?

Not knowing what else to do—you could tell that even Bobby wasn't sure how to handle this—we continued toward the door; but when we were almost to it, she stepped in front of us. She was smiling, and clearly she was not going to let us pass.

"Where the fuck did she come from?" Keith whispered.

She was wearing a little cape—a gray one. It was hot that day, but she was wearing a cape. She was crazy, that was obvious, or she wouldn't be here. She wore a dress, basically the kind all the young women wore on the *passeggia* in the evening at the waterfront—the kind they'd been wearing for decades—and she was pretty, though her eyes were a little far apart and her lipstick wasn't on quite right. She was wearing a little cap, too—a cap made from the same gray cloth as the cape. She didn't seem scared of us, and she didn't seem frightened by what had happened to Marco. She seemed concerned, sure, but calm, as if this happened all the time, boys and arrows and screams and wounds.

What do you do with a calm crazy woman standing in your way in an old building? We weren't sure. We just knew we needed to get Marco out of there and to a real hospital.

"*Voglio aiutare*," she asked calmly.

"What did she say," Bobby asked.

"She wants to help," I answered.

"Right," Keith snorted. "He needs a doctor."

"Yes, he does," Bobby said.

Marco was staring at her as if in a trance—as if this were all a dream. He was in shock, and in shock you can be awake but dreaming, too.

"Marco?" I said, and he didn't answer.

She was looking at him as if she knew him—which made no sense. How could Marco know her? *He* wasn't acting like he did.

"Let me help you," she said in Italian, and Bobby didn't ask for a translation.

She came over to them, and Bobby stepped back.

"What are you doing?" Keith said to Bobby. "She's crazy. We need to get out of here."

Bobby was staring at her as if in a dream, too.

She was close enough to us that you could hear the rustle of her dress, smell her perfume, even smell the wool of her cape and cap—as if it were winter and they were wet.

She took Marco's good arm—Marco let her, and so did Bobby—and led Marco to the corner. We followed.

There was indeed a table there, and it wasn't empty. It was covered with all sorts of things, the very things I'd imagined had once been on tables here. Hadn't Keith seen them? First-aid things, gauze and bandages and needles and bottles of tablets and rubber tubing and thread for stitching.

"Those weren't there—" Keith started to say, but didn't finish.

The woman was pulling the table out into the light, and we were helping. She sat Marco down on a stool—the one she'd been sitting on in the shadows, I guess—and inspected the arrow, where it entered his neck above his T-shirt. With scissors from the table she cut away his shirt, and then, giving him something to bite down on—a thick wad of gauze—she pulled the arrow out carefully, watching the angle of it.

Marco should have been screaming, at least crying, but that would have embarrassed him; and besides, she was right next to him, her perfume in his nose, the smell of her clothes, too, and her touch, the touch of someone who seemed to care, even if she was crazy. He was looking up at her puzzled, but grateful.

She had a glass of water on the table, too—perhaps because she'd been thirsty, sitting there in the abandoned building all day. Who was she? Why was she here? Why did she have a table covered with first-aid things? Were there men, migrants from the south, living in these olive groves and she wasn't crazy at all; she was married to one of them and sat here in case one of them got hurt? Or was she crazy as a loon and did this because she thought she was someone else and was waiting for someone who'd never come? But if she was crazy, where was her family? Where did she live? Why did they let her do it? Alone in an abandoned building where men—men more dangerous than us—could stumble in one day and maybe hurt her?

She gave Marco three pills to take with the water, which he did, and did not try to stitch up the perfect little hole left by the arrow.

"*Ha bisogno di un'iniezione*," she said.

"He'll need an injection," Keith's friend—whose Italian was obviously better than the brothers'—said.

"Sure," Bobby said. He was looking impatient, as if the mystery of the woman had been only a moment's dream, and getting out of this place was what really mattered — which, for Marco's sake, was true.

"*Dovete portarlo subito in ospedale,*" she said.

"Hospital, yes," Bobby said before anyone could translate it.

Then she said something that stopped my heart. She looked at Keith and Bobby, who were side by side now, cocked her heard just a little, and asked gently:

"*Perché avete rimosso la testa della statua?*"

Keith and Bobby had no idea what she was saying, and it took me a second to find the courage to tell them.

"She wants — she wants to know why you took its head…the statue's head."

Keith jumped, and even Bobby, calm as he usually was, stepped back.

"What?"

She was waiting for an answer. Then she said: "*Perche? Perche la testa di una donna morta tanti anni fa e cosi triste nei suoi ultimi anni….*"

I looked at Keith's friend, but the Italian was beyond him.

"*Why?*" I began--wishing I weren't the one to have to do it. "*Why the head…of a woman dead all these years….and so sad during her final days….*"

Keith was looking at Bobby. Bobby was looking back. They'd both lost some color in their faces.

Keith said, "No one could have see us — it was night. It was--"

"Shut up, asshole," Bobby answered. "Who cares if she saw us?"

As Bobby guided Marco through the door, and Keith-- looking afraid and angry and ashamed — muttered what sounded like, "Bitch!", everyone followed, but I trailed behind. I couldn't help it. I couldn't stop looking at her, and neither could Marco. Even as Bobby pushed him through the door, he was looking back at her as if he did know her. A chill ran down my neck.

"*Lo conosce?*" I heard myself say to her. "You know him?"

"*Si*," she answered, her eyes on Marco. "*Lo conosco da sempre.*"

Yes. I know him always.

I'd never heard the expression before, and would never hear it again. *To know someone* always.

What she said next, her eyes still on Marco, I would also never forget:

"*Grazie. Per me lui è un dono.*"

Thank you for the gift he is.

The chill did not go away. I walked quickly to the door, not looking back. I didn't want to see what was in her eyes, even if it looked like love.

Afterwards, the doctors said we'd done the right thing not letting Marco walk back to my house, but simply having him sit at the foot of the statue, keeping him awake, while I, since my Italian was better, ran to the nearest house on the path home and had them call my dad, who came in our car and drove Marco to the hospital in La Spezia.

The doctors also complimented whoever had removed the arrow and given Marco antibiotics — an old-fashioned kind, sulfonamides (Marco had one in his pocket still). When we said a woman in the old German hospital had done it, they thought we were drunk, I'm sure. We insisted. A woman had been there. "Well," they said, "she must have been a nurse. She knew what angle to remove it on, and the danger. The tip of the arrow was near the carotid artery. If she hadn't removed it and the boy had fallen on it…."

A month later, when Marco's wound had healed, my parents said what I'd known they would say — that I had to go to the man in the villa, who indeed did own the old hospital and all the land up from the cove, and apologize in person. I was, after all, the son of a Naval officer and therefore an ambassador from America, though apparently not a very good one; and I needed to try to fix the damage. My dad would go with me, it was decided, and that was because Keith and his brother weren't going. They were back in school in Rome; and, rather than having them apologize in person to the owner, Commander Speer had paid the man a very generous amount according to my dad, and also returned the head of the statue, which Bobby had been keeping under his bed and Keith had decorated with some of his sister's lipstick. He was of course also paying for Marco's medical bills since these would have been a hardship for any Vecchia Lerici family.

You could tell from my mother's look what she was thinking when she heard that Commander Speer wasn't making his boys apologize in person. Maybe this is how fathers from families like that behaved, but this was not going to be how we were going to behave.

The owner told my parents what he'd told Commander Speer--that a face-to-face apology wasn't necessary, that he didn't need additional monetary compensation, that an apology on the phone was quite sufficient; but my father insisted. He and I would visit the owner the next weekend.

The same day my dad spoke to the owner by phone, I ran into Marco at the wharf. He had his fishing pole and I had mine; and my real friends—the ones from the "right" families— weren't with me because they didn't like to fish. It was that simple. Stamp collecting, maybe, and playing war in the olive groves, and soccer; but not fishing, especially from the wharf or *passeggiata* rocks, where people could see you and think you were a technical-school kid. "You're an American," Carlo said. "You can get away with it." I wasn't sure exactly what I was getting away with, but I went ahead and fished, and that day Marco was there.

When I told him what I had to do, that my dad would be accompanying me to apologize, he said, "If I go with you, maybe your father will not have to." I could tell he felt bad about the windows, but I knew that wasn't the main reason he offered. We were still friends—even if friends usually don't get you shot in the neck with an arrow—and that meant something to him, as it did to me. He didn't ask whether Keith and Bobby would be going. He knew I'd have mentioned it if they were. He didn't even seem angry at Keith. Boys like Keith—and arrows falling from the sky—were to be expected, and you accepted them and went on with your life.

He was right, it turned out. If he came, my parents agreed, my father wouldn't need to. "That's very kind of Marco," my mother said. A part of me was of course thinking that if the victim of the shooting was with me, the owner might not be as angry, but I certainly wasn't going to admit it.

When we reached the statue, it was still headless. The head hadn't been put back on yet. Could you even do that? Could you glue cement? She might be headless forever, and Keith and Bobby would have gotten away with murder again.

Instead of taking the gravel fork to the hospital, we took the one to the left, toward the villa, a much longer walk.

It wasn't a grand villa, like the Tincani or the Musetti in Romito, but it was fine enough. The man who answered the doorbell was business-like, but not stern. He seemed maybe 30—handsome, in good shape, with a wide-open shirt and a gold chain around his neck—but he was obviously the owner. He didn't have a butler or maid to answer the door, and he didn't seem to need one. He had money, but he wasn't old, and that kept him from being stuffy, the way the owners of the bigger villas often were.

He shook my hand first; and when I introduced Marco— "*Voglio presentarle un mio amico: si chiama Matteotti Marco*" —he shook Marco's hand and looked at him for a long time. "You are the one struck by the arrow?" he asked at last. The *carabinieri*, we knew, had told him what had happened—at least the major points. This was not a world where people sued if something happened to them—something that was their own fault—on someone else's property, so the owner had not retained a lawyer. A boy had been shot with an arrow, a dangerous wound, but had survived, and that was what mattered.

"*Si*," Marco answered.

The man led us to the travertine-marble living room, where we all sat down, the man at ease, Marco and I nervous. The man didn't want us nervous. He smiled at us as we settled in, and soon we were feeling calmer.

"Matteotti?" he began in Italian to Marco. "The Matteotti of Lerici?"

"*Si*," Marco said again.

The man looked at Marco awhile longer, and then said, "I think we are cousins."

Marco smiled. To have a cousin this wealthy, and to have such a cousin admit he was a cousin—that had made the trip worth it already. Maybe not the arrow, but certainly the trip.

Marco's Italian was, of course, better than mine, but I didn't want him to have to do the apologizing. My parents wouldn't have wanted it, and I didn't want it either. I was here to ask for the man's forgiveness and to offer to pay for my share (and Marco's, too) of the broken windows; and if I was going to go through this unpleasantness, I wanted some credit for it. That Marco had come along was his gift to me, and I didn't need any others.

In the best Italian I could, I explained that we had come to apologize. The man, whose name was Paolo—Paolo Pastore--was gracious enough not to interrupt, but to let me speak, even if it was a tediously slow and halting speech. But even after one sentence—a simple "I am (which Marco graciously corrected to "We are—") here to apologize for breaking the windows of your hospital"—I got into trouble and Marco had to help with some of the words. The owner just listened.

"We were very inconsiderate," I said, "and hope you will forgive us, *Signore*."

"I do," he answered.

"We would like to remunerate you—we would like to compensate you--for the windows; and not only for our share, but for any that might not be covered by the amount provided by the families of the other three boys."

"That will not be necessary," the man said, as if following

his own script, too.

"Are you certain, *Signore*, that--"

"Yes," he interrupted gently, "I am certain. I would have preferred that the windows remained intact, simply because buildings deserve respect, as do people; but I will not be spending money on replacing the glass. The hospital will probably be torn down when we eventually sell the land. We were more disturbed by the damage...to the statue."

At that moment--and as his "we" made me wonder whether he was married or had a brother or had his parents living with him--a young woman appeared with orange sodas, real straw straws and a plate of cookies. So he *did* have a maid, even if she hadn't answered the door. She wasn't dressed like a maid--she wore an ordinary dress--but she certainly acted like one. She wouldn't look at us, as if she were there only to deliver the drinks and cookies — the way a maid would. Maybe, I told myself, he didn't care about formalities like uniforms.

"Thank you," he said to her. "These are two of the boys from the hospital." She nodded, but did not look up, and in a moment had returned to the kitchen.

We drank from our bottles and we ate our cookies, and Paolo watched us, seemingly pleased.

"I hear," he said at last, "that someone helped you with the arrow. I'm very glad to hear that. Time is often of the essence."

"Yes," I answered. I thought Marco might say something then, too — about his famous arrow — but he didn't. He wanted the conversation to be mine.

"The arrow was close to a — an artery," I added, "so it had to be removed carefully."

"The police did not give me many details. I don't believe they had many. Was it someone from the coast road who stopped and helped you?"

I looked at Marco and Marco looked back. We'd assumed — everyone had — that he knew the woman in the hospital, or at least knew of her existence, and that by now he'd heard the entire story about the arrow. But if he didn't know the woman, and the *carabinieri* hadn't known the details....

I didn't know where to begin.

I said:

"The woman was there in the hospital, and she was very helpful...."

He frowned, and was silent, as if trying to decide something.

"That must have been Gianna," he said at last.

Who was Gianna?

"Gianna is my sister."

We nodded. That certainly explained it. He had a crazy sister.

"But she took the arrow out of him?" This seemed to puzzle him.

"*Si*," Marco said. The memory of the woman who'd touched him, the one whose perfume he'd smelled, who'd looked at him with what could have been love—the woman who, it now turned out, was this man's sister—made him suddenly talkative. "She was very good at it, the doctors said. She knew exactly the angle at which to remove it."

The man was still frowning. "I—" he began, but then stopped. A door in the direction of the kitchen—a door to the outside, with a spring on it—slammed shut, and this seemed to set him free. The maid was gone. We could talk honestly now. He sighed again, and it was as if he were thinking: *Why not? These boys—especially the one with the arrow—who might be my cousin—deserve to know it, do they not?*

"Yes, that would have been my sister, Gianna," he was saying. "She goes to the hospital almost every day and sits there on a stool and listens for voices."

It was just what I'd imagined.

"She has emotional problems," he was saying gently. "She receives medication for them, and going to the hospital every day makes her happy. That Gianna didn't mention her role in what happened does not surprise me. She doesn't tell me everything—and I am not sure her memory is always accurate--but I am very happy she was able to help. It must--it must have made her feel very good to be able to help...."

He was, something told me, leaving things out. You could tell. He was speaking carefully, as if walking around a pond, trying not to step in the water.

Then he sighed. *Why not?* he was telling himself again. He liked us. That was obvious, and, again, Marco was probably family. *These are boys*, he was thinking, *and perhaps someday, when they are grown, this story will mean something to them, just as it has meant something to us.*

As he began to tell the rest of it, he gazed out the window that overlooked the hills and the cove; and except for once or twice, when Marco had to repeat or rephrase things for me, he did not look at us.

His sister had done this — gone to the hospital every day — ever since their mother had died, he explained. Their mother had died five years ago, ten years after the war.

His sister went to the hospital to think of their mother, whom she missed terribly and without whom, in many ways, she could not find life worth living. Which was why the doctors had her on medication, and why Paolo had to make sure she took it dutifully. Was he worried about her when she visited the hospital? No, it was safe there — we were the first people ever to discover her — and she always returned from it contented, in less despair.

Their mother, who was from Lerici, had felt and acted that way, too--in the years just after the war, in her final years of life. She too had started going to the abandoned German hospital soon after the war ended. As her daughter would after her death, she had set up a table and put medical supplies on it, as if waiting for wounded soldiers to come.

She had been a nurse during the war, one to whom a terrible thing had happened. Toward the end of the war she had been conscripted by the Germans to work at that hospital, a hospital for German officers. Because it was at the end of the war and because Hitler held *il Duce* in such contempt, blaming the Italians for many of his problems, only Germans could be

103

treated in that hospital. Italian soldiers—even officers--would have to fend for themselves in whatever local clinic they could find, or in the overcrowded, undersupplied hospital near La Spezia many kilometers to the north.

Their mother was married, and had already given birth to both Paolo and his sister, who were 15 and 10 respectively. Her husband—their father—had been born in Sarzana, a town just inland from Lerici, and they had met at a procession for St. Erasmus, Lerici's patron saint, when they were twenty.

Their father was a foot soldier in the Italian army now, while their mother attended to German officers—and only German officers--at the hospital. The children were being taken care of by their aunt, their mother's sister.

One night their father, Emilio Pastore, appeared at the door of the hospital. He had been wounded—in his stomach—on the road from Parma to Lerici, where he hoped to see his wife. He had not been shot by an American or other Ally soldier, but a German, a German officer, and he had been shot because he had refused to do what the German had ordered—namely, that he turn around and return to Parma. Emilio had escaped and, bleeding, had made his way to the clinic in Lerici, only to discover that it had burned down four nights before. He had then caught a ride on an armored personnel carrier to La Spezia, but his wound was severe and he knew that he would not make it that far, or that even if he did, he might not survive long enough to see his wife, who was, after all, right here at this hospital.

When he appeared at the hospital's door, supported by two Italian soldiers--the infection in his stomach spreading like fire through dead grass—he barely recognized the world around him, but asked for Nurse Pastore. When she arrived, German guards would neither let her leave the building to help him nor let him enter to be ministered to, since the hospital was for German officers only.

Their mother had pleaded with the guards, and even with the director of the hospital, who had arrived to find out what the commotion was about. But he refused her as well, making her return to her patients even though she cried and hit at the guards. Three hours later word reached her through another nurse that her husband had died in front of the hospital, on the earth, and that his body was still there because the two Italian soldiers with him had been arrested and taken away.

Their mother never recovered. After the war, she lived in San Terenzo so that she might be closer to the hospital, which was soon stripped by thieves of its cots and tables and wiring and everything else of worth. When everything was gone, and no one cared about the building anymore, she began to visit it, to visit it every day, sitting at a little card table she hid in the shadows when she left, arranging her first-aid materials on it, waiting for her husband to come. Her sister continued to help her with the children, and when Paolo was 25, he bought a shoe store for very little money, made a success of it, bought five more and did so well that in the very year that their mother died he was able to buy the land in the cove, the villa and the abandoned hospital, because it had mattered to her so much--

--just as it came to matter to his sister, who, not three months after their mother died, began to visit the hospital each day, too, using the same folding table and chair and what she brought with her for the table. She had always been an emotional child; but when their mother died, she seemed to disappear — to become, in her own mind, their mother — and if this was what God wanted from their lives, he as owner of the land and buildings and she the one who carried on their mother's vigil, how could he argue?

At his sister's urging, he had commissioned a statue of their mother--an honest one, one that did not hide her sadness, and the damage to it mattered, he repeated in closing, much more to him than the windows.

Marco and I were staring. We had stopped nodding long ago. Everything made sense now, and yet we had no idea what to say. "We're sorry." "It must have been difficult." "How terrible a war is." Nothing would sound right.

Paolo was looking at us, but I saw no regret — regret that he had shared such a story with two boys. Something had made him share it, and that something still made the sharing feel right.

"Please thank your sister for helping me," Marco said.

"I certainly will," the man answered, and then no one said a thing.

When the silence had gone on too long — when all we could do, and all he could, too, was smile--we got up and thanked him. He said, "You're entirely welcome," and we were heading toward the front door when we heard the kitchen door open and close again and footsteps approaching. We had reached the fireplace mantle — one with photographs on it--and of course wanted to see them, to see a picture of their mother and father, if they had them.

"You will find a picture of our mother on that mantle," Paolo said, as if reading my thoughts, "if you are interested."

We both were, said so, and looked; and the only photograph of a woman on the mantle made us stop.

The footsteps from the kitchen had arrived, and Paolo was saying, "*Ragazzi*, this is my sister, Gianna."

We turned. It was the "maid."

This was his sister?

This was not the woman in the hospital.

The woman in the picture on the mantelpiece was.

I looked at Marco and Marco looked back, and somehow Paolo knew. Perhaps he'd felt it one night. Perhaps he'd seen it in his sister's face one day, or on many days, when she'd returned from the hospital or was about to leave for it. *That she'd met someone there. That she hadn't really been alone.*

"No —" he said, shaking his head. "It was Gianna you met — who helped you. Gianna, you remember the boys, yes?"

The young woman, her eyes crazy — this was the reason she didn't look at people, I knew — glanced at us quickly and shook her head. "No, Paolo. I do not remember them." She was holding another plate of cookies. "Would you like more, *ragazzi*?

Would the boys like more cookies, Paolo?"

"Gianna is the one you met. She just doesn't remember — she is on medication--and because of the shadows and the commotion, you do not remember either. It is understandable. Marco was shot in the neck, a dangerous wound. The light, the commotion...."

Neither of us said a thing. I looked back at the picture on the mantle — at the pretty face with wide-set eyes — and could almost smell her again. I wondered how often she'd gotten her lipstick wrong in the craziness of war, the wounded and dying soldiers, and whether she'd been wearing lipstick the night her husband had come to the hospital.

"Thank you for coming over, boys," Paolo was saying, hurrying us toward the door. "That was very kind of you. Your families should be proud."

Marco was ahead of me. As we reached the door, Paolo touched my back to stop me, and in English — with a thick Italian accent — said, for me and me alone:

"The boy's name — the one who shot Marco — is 'Speer,' correct?"

"Yes."

"Is that name German?"

I didn't know why he was asking.

"Yes," I said in English too. "Yes, it is."

"Is his father an officer?"

"Yes," I said, still not understanding, but then seeing it at last.

Paolo was staring out through the window to the hills and cove once more, as if in a dream.

"Then Marco is indeed my cousin," he said quietly, still in English. "Wounded men. It could not be otherwise. A story needs an ending. Please tell him."

And then he added, perhaps to me — perhaps not:

"Sometimes I hear a great clock ticking, *ragazzo*. That is the only way I know to say it."

As we took the road back to my house, I thought of our hunchback teacher, how he had made what had happened possible, and wondered whether he somehow knew. I thought about the woman he cared for, whether she was still alive, or whether she called to him only from his heart. I wondered how far someone might go to hold onto what they loved.

Marco was asking what the owner had said to me in English. I answered that he'd thanked me for coming, and that he'd said something strange about a big clock, but mainly that he'd wanted to show off his English, too.

Marco didn't believe me. I wasn't lying well.

"That woman in the photograph — "

"Yes," I answered.

"Wasn't *that* the woman?"

"I don't know," I lied again. "It could have been her or it could have been his sister, I'm really not sure. He is right. There was a lot of commotion, and the light was bad…."

"Is she still there?"

"Who?"

"That woman."

"I don't think so," I said. "I think she is gone now."

Marco stared at me as we walked. He knew I wasn't telling him everything; but he knew too that he would, just like me, have to make of what had happened that day in the hospital a story that somehow made sense to him, one that he could live with forever.

VIII

MARY

...In the winter of that same year the boy wrote a story about the witch who had poisoned his cat without meaning to. When the hunchback didn't seem to notice that he was writing in class, the boy dropped his pen twice and rustled his notebook pages until the man looked over at him, smiled and nodded. The boy understood: Even if their teacher wasn't looking at him, the man knew; and this helped the boy to write.

In the spring, when the school had its essay competition about Jesus, the boy wrote about how being gentle, kind and reasonable was difficult in a world where people thought it was a weakness to be that way. The boy's tutor – which the boy had had since his first summer there – helped him translate it, and make it better, and the essay tied for first place. It was only fair, the boy's mother pointed out to everyone at his father's work, that it be a tie. A visitor to the village, after all, shouldn't be the only winner – especially one with a tutor to help him. One of the judges was Professore Brigola, who, though he must have known about the tutor, wrote a note on the boy's essay for the other judges to see: "This is a persuasive argument for love and reason, and the author writes with true heart."

* * *

When the boy grew sick the next year and his parents had to take him back to the States, the village and everything he had known there became a story – one that he could not be sure belonged to him, though he would try to write it. When, many years later, he was grown and married, with children of his own, he returned to the village to look for his teacher, to tell him that he had, just as the man had wished, continued to write; that indeed his stories – better ones than he'd written in school, of course--had been published; and that he had one of them to give to him. It was one his teacher might like. It was about that drowned poet and a strange, pretty girl the boy had known in the village just before his family left--a girl who had memorized all of the

109

poet's poems, too.

But the hunchback was gone. When the boy found his best friend – who was living with his own wife and children in one of the castle towns not far away – Gianluca said, "I am sorry, Brad, but Brigola jumped from the castle wall in despair ten years ago because that woman in San Terenzo married another." As Gianluca said this, Maurizio, his other best friend, who was there for dinner too, shook his head and later, as they were leaving, whispered: "The witches poisoned him. He was a good person, so they poisoned him. That's what my uncle always said. He threw himself from the castle, yes, but only because he was dying from poison."

The boy did not believe this. Their teacher would not have killed himself. From others in the village he heard that the hunchback had drowned years ago, boating in the bay in June, when it is always dangerous to boat or swim; and also that he had been killed only a few years ago by students from Parma, who, coming to the olive groves during the summer to shoot drugs into their arms, had found him walking on Via San Giuseppe one evening and attacked him for his money. Even the Contessa Musetti, who couldn't think well now, had a story: "He became a cat. Or was it a lizard? I don't remember. It's a secret, but you may tell your mother – but only her." And then, as the American boy was about to leave, a man at the hotel said: "Brigola? He died of tuberculosis ten years after your family left, Signore. I do not know why there are so many rumors, except that he was a man who knew things a man perhaps should not know, and so he attracted them. Besides, this is a village of stories, and sometimes, Signore, it is the strangest stories that are the truest. In any event, hunchbacks never live long."

The boy did not know what to do. He had, he saw now, been waiting all this time to bring his teacher a story. He had, in fact (he saw now), been writing all these years for him, for the man who had not gotten mad at him that day in class and who had, for reasons the boy would never understand, wanted him to write. As if writing made life worth living. As if it led to the truth, to the power of Love and Reason. What use was it, the writing, the publishing of stories, now that the man who had helped him feel what needed to be felt was gone? The boy could do nothing but go home. And there, one day, at his desk, as if it were a story being told by another, he thought of Mary, her drowned husband, of the red doorways and the nurse and the strange girl on the beach, and of a hunchback who, cursed with the living soul of a long-dead poet, loved a woman he could never have; and the boy felt this and could write again.

IX

HEART OF HEARTS

Dearest Mary,
I am this moment arrived in Lerici, where I am
necessarily detained, waiting the furniture...; and as
the sea has been calm, and the wind fair, I may expect
it every moment. It would not do to leave affairs here
in an impiccio, great as is my anxiety to see you. How
are you, my best love? How have you sustained the
trials of the journey? Answer me this question, and
how my little babe and C are.
--Percy Bysshe Shelley, to Mary Shelley.

Whether Lerici was, as local legend claimed, the village where Mary Shelley dreamed the dream that became her novel — *Frankenstein* — that book about a doctor's monster--Mary's husband, Percy, did drown there in a summer storm. It might have been a design flaw in his boat (he'd just purchased it in Genoa), or the boat was rammed by thieves, or he was murdered because of his politics (he was a champion of the common man). No one knows; but drown he did, washing up on a beach near Lerici, where a young woman found him and kept him alive until he died at last in her arms. That at least was the story the village told of Percy's last moments; and it was the story I'd come to believe, too.

Mary, Percy and their good friend, the moody poet Lord Byron, had been living in a dark, damp villa on Lerici's coastal road. This is certainly true. And so is this: That Mary had always felt a foreboding about the villa — one that, were Lerici the village where she dreamed her dream, found life in the novel she finished just before her husband's death. And that Percy, a sensitive young man, had felt a foreboding, too, seeing his double — his *doppelganger*--in the village shortly before his death, and also, rising from the moonlit waters of Lerici one night, the vision of a child — one with open arms and a joyful smile.

Their villa was no longer there when my family arrived more than a century later. But on a hill above where their villa had been sat a plain, white, stucco hotel built in the '50s called The Hotel Byron, and in town was another hotel, the Hotel Shelley. The villagers, I'd soon learn, still told the story of Mary and Percy and their two dead children. How their third child survived and was great comfort to Mary at her husband's death, though he didn't seem to have his parents' talents and he died without having children himself. And how, because Percy wasn't always faithful (believing, as he and Byron and their friends did, in the "freest" of love) he may have sired out of wedlock near Lerici a secret child, one that did *not* die.

I'd hear even stranger things, though history books confirm them: Mary, before he was cremated, was given his heart, which she kept with her until she died; and the plaque over his ashes, which were buried in Rome because he requested it, bore the Latin words "*Cor Cordium*" — "*Heart of Hearts*"--words only a good friend would choose.

I heard these things from my tutor, who held his cigarettes so tightly he crushed them sometimes; from our *Professore* Brigola; and from the parents and aunts and cousins of my best friends. It didn't really matter which were true and which weren't. They were a story, not unlike the ones I'd begun to write myself, caught in the village's magic. What mattered was that the village found them true and so *made* them true.

My second year of middle school became my third. The Speer family was transferred to Naples; Marco never mentioned the old German hospital again; and I avoided going anywhere near it...even though I dreamed, more than once, that it was me — not a dead soldier, not even Marco (though he did deserve it) — that the nurse loved.

I heard another story, too. Not about the Shelleys, but about the three women, always three—two old and one young--whom the village called *streghe*—witches--but with respect and gratitude. And how at each fishing season these three women blessed, with whatever spells they knew, the village's fishing nets--which had been dyed a dark red with dye from two sea animals, two kinds of *Murex* snails, that lived here. This dye, legend said, was beautiful and aromatic to the fish, and by its beauty and perfume lured them to the nets. It was the same dye that the Romans, our teacher explained (though without speaking of witches and the luring of fish), had used to color their royal robes, just like the Greeks and Etruscans.

I had a seashell collection. I'd started it years ago on another ocean where my father had been stationed, and my parents had always encouraged it. You couldn't take your friends with you when you moved, but you could take what you'd collected. The two purple-dye *Murexes* were among my favorites, their story important enough to me (the Roman and Greek parts anyway) that I'd written it neatly on a card and placed it in the box that held a dozen specimens of them, as well as the other shells I'd collected in the cove and from the fishing nets of the Lerici fishermen, who told me I should take them.

I didn't make a connection between these stories. I didn't know they were the same story. I hadn't yet met Livia, the girl of the cove where the fishing nets were sometimes dyed--a girl who wasn't a ghost, but perhaps should have been one--and, because I hadn't met her, the village didn't need to tell me. My own part in the story hadn't started, so there was nothing yet for the village to say.

Even at fifteen, the boys and girls of the village didn't date. This wasn't America. It wasn't just that it was a Catholic world, or that boys and girls were separated in middle school. It was the *spirit* of the village, I'd decided—a spirit that let everyone know who they were, gave them a place, and by doing this kept them innocent. The older boys were never mean to the younger ones. No one ever made fun of our hunchback teacher. And mothers kissed their 15-year-olds in front of the school building without their children getting too embarrassed. Only innocence could explain this, I told myself.

This didn't, of course, keep my friends from trying to set me up with girls (even if the idea of my being in love with a girl was so absurd to them, as I'm sure it was, that they laughed so hard they cried). It wasn't that I didn't like girls — I always went crazy looking too long at the lips of a pretty girl, or her bare arms, or her body in a bathing suit. It was just that we never really got that close--physically, I mean, to girls, and never *privately* — and the girls were shy and stayed with their friends too. But up to that point I'd liked other things just as much as girls: My books, some full of adventures, some about the sea; my seashell collection (all neatly labeled with their Latin names); the stories I'd started to write; playing war with my friends in the olive groves; getting into trouble with witches, crying babies, long-dead nurses or Navy brats; or better yet, sitting on an Etruscan wall by myself and watching the lizards I'd come to love ever since they'd slept with me — and who watched me back.

They imagined I couldn't possibly like a girl with dark hair or olive skin, like their sisters. I was an American and disturbingly white and blue-eyed, with red hair and freckles, looking, I'm sure, more like a speckled ghost than a boy. Because this was their thinking, Gianluca, Maurizio and Carlo insisted on recommending girls with blonde hair (especially ones with braids), girls with blue or green eyes, girls with a German mother or father, and girls with freckles — as if the only girl I'd be interested in had to look like *me*. This narrowed the field to almost nothing; but there were a few candidates, and my friends kept pushing and teasing: "See that girl over there with the braids? Her father is German, from Lombardy. She is right for you, yes?" Gianluca would ask, pretending to swoon, his long eyelashes fluttering. "No," Carlo would counter. "There is that girl in *Professoressa* Piatta's class — the one with *occhii azzurri* — who certainly must already be dreaming of the *barba rossa* Brad will grow when he is a man. It may scare her, that hair, since it is the sign of the devil certainly; but the devil does make a passionate lover, my uncle says." Maurizio, blue-eyed himself and very red-faced when he got embarrassed, which happened easily, would chime in with a sympathetic, "Be kind to Brad—if he does not want to burden himself thinking about girls, he should not have to." Then the other two would tease *him*. "Tell us what girl *you* dream about at night, Maurizio. Does she have a protractor?" And Maurizio would turn redder. He thought only of geometry, drafting and architecture, we knew, never girls.

I did dream for a week about an actress—a feisty brunette my age who was very popular. I'd seen her in three movies imported from America and wanted very much to set out on adventures with her, but also to find out, when we could make time for it between (or during) our adventures, what kissing was like—since I'd had so little experience with it. But then the seashells began calling again. They were more real than any girl on a movie screen. And we hadn't yet, my friends and I, finished building our fort in the olive groves not far from the huts of the sad old women, the witches. And there were all those stories to write, too—stories about those three witches, another witch who lived in the castle and spat at the tourists, the vipers that sometimes swarmed on the hills at night (I'd seen them myself), the man at the wharf with no throat who spoke by spitting air, our teacher whose lisp softened everything he said, and our maid, a woman even older than the witches and who had one blue eye and one white and smiled at me as if she knew something I did not.

I don't remember who it was who first mentioned the girl in the cove. Maybe more than one of my friends did, conspiring. Or maybe Marco, as I fished with him on the rocks one day, though he would not have put it as, "Boy, do I have a girl for you." He would have said, "People talk about a girl, a strange girl who…." Or perhaps it was Terotto. I like to think it was him. Terotto was a friend from middle school that my other friends also knew, but one that we never really hung out with because his family, like Marco's, wasn't the "professional class" of my other friends' families. His father was a navigator out at sea most of the year, and his mother, to make extra money, was a seamstress. He missed his father, I could tell. He missed him very much. You could hear it in his voice — like a story or spell he couldn't break free of.

If it was Terotto — tall and quiet and, even if sad sometimes, always dignified — he'd have said, "There is a girl who lives in Vecchia Lerici, old town, just below the castle. She plays in the cove on the other side of the castle, where the fishing nets are dyed, and she makes strange designs in the sand, using — and this is why I have thought to mention her--seashells to make them. Have you ever been to that cove?" He would not have said, as Gianluca or Carlo would, teasing me, "We've got a girlfriend for you. She's *strana*, maybe *pazza*, maybe even *strega*, but she's sure right for you!"

The first time I saw Livia, I didn't know it was her. Someone had mentioned "a girl at that cove," but I hadn't gone there until months later — taking the little tunnel at the base of the castle (the only way to get from the wharf to that cove) to look for seashells after a little storm, one that had only sunk a dinghy or two, and to swim if I felt like it. My parents didn't care where I went in Lerici. They trusted the sea unless they had a reason not to, and it was hard not to trust it there. The Mediterranean doesn't have much of a tide, the waves are tiny in summer, and the water was crystal clear. There were no sharks or stingrays. And besides, they believed — even if they didn't know why — that the village would watch over me.

As I headed down the stone stairs to the cove, I could see two figures at the edge of the water, maybe ten feet from it. I first thought that someone--the girl--had almost drowned, and that the boy, a big boy almost as tall as my father, had rescued her. But when I looked harder I saw she was sitting up, as if she'd only been asleep, and how they were sitting together like friends. Maybe, I told myself, he'd just woken her up. He was older anyway--18, maybe even 20 --and their bodies weren't moving when they talked the way boyfriend and girlfriend would've moved.

There was this, too: The girl couldn't have been drowning. She couldn't have been swimming. She was wearing a dress.

And this: There were patterns — five or six of them — on the sand, even closer to the water's edge — three on my side of the boy and girl and three on the other side. They were like the patterns little kids make on the sand, using anything they can find — pebbles, shells, seaweed and tiny pieces of driftwood — but they also weren't: They were perfectly spaced — each about ten feet from the next, the girl and boy in the middle, and they were too neat to be a kid's. One triangular, one a circle, one a star.

I squinted so hard at the patterns — trying to understand them — I nearly forgot the boy and girl. I knew seashells, and the designs certainly looked as if they were made from seashells, nothing else — no pebbles, driftwood, seaweed at all.

I remembered the girl and boy again and squinted at them instead. Both were dark-haired, the boy olive-skinned, the girl much paler, her hair pitch black against her white skin.

The boy stood up, the girl very awake and looking up at him as he walked to a spot much higher in the sand. Another girl was sitting there, waiting patiently--one his own age, in a bathing suit, on a blanket. *This* was his girlfriend — that was obvious--but he did know the other girl, the one at sea's edge. A sister? A cousin? His girlfriend's sister? But why was she wearing a dress at the beach?

She was up on her knees now, making something in the sand. Another pattern? I was remembering them now, Terotto's words, if he was the one who'd really said them: *There is a girl who lives in Vecchia Lerici, under the castle. She makes strange designs in the sand, and she makes them with seashells.*

She had, I could see, gathered shells — yes, shells--from the beach and put them in a pile behind her. She was choosing from the pile what she needed. She was making very carefully what she made, hesitating a second before she made a choice, and another second before she put the shell on the sand. I'd never seen anyone—anyone our age anyway—doing anything like this, and I couldn't stop staring.

Had she made the other six patterns today, or were they old; but if they were old, why were they still in perfect shape? They were near the water line, where people walked and children played.

I wasn't going to walk out there myself and interrupt her. I was too self-conscious, and, even though I wanted very much to see her designs, I also just wanted to watch her. But when a German tourist suddenly appeared in the tunnel behind me, walking toward me, I returned to the wharf and whatever seashells I might find on the tables where the fisherwomen laid out the day's catch and smiled their toothless smiles, letting me take whatever I wanted.

It was very strange, the girl and the boy who knew her and what she was making in the sand—and how familiar it all was somehow, too. I thought about her a lot over the next couple of days because I had so many questions, but I didn't go back. There were things to do with my friends; Marco wanted to fish; and I had exams and family outings. Besides, I didn't think I had a right to answers that weren't my business.

The next time I saw her I'd actually gone to the cove to be alone. Carlo was being bossier than usual—his mother had what might be cancer, and it scared him, and when he was scared he got bossy—and Gianluca had the flu, and Maurizio had taken a trip to Pisa with his uncle. And I just wasn't in the mood to go to the rocks to fish with *Professore* Brigola or Marco.

I was wearing shorts—all the boys wore shorts even when it was cold—and if I wanted to swim in the cove, I could swim in them. I sometimes swam; I sometimes didn't. It depended on how cold the water was and how self-conscious I was feeling, whether there were people around, whether I just wanted to pick up shells on the beach, and maybe look them up in my book, which was in French but which I could make my way through well enough since one Romance language is a lot like another.

I had my book with me, my diving mask, and a blanket, and as soon I saw how smooth the water was, just a gentle breeze, no waves at all really, and how clear it was, I put my blanket down, my book on it, looked around, saw no one, and walked into the water. I liked using my mask because with it I could watch the two kinds of *Murex* snail crawling peacefully across the sand in the shallow water of any cove. It was like a dream, the peaceful kind—the kind you imagine Heaven must be like—where you can forget who you are, your body, your family, everything in the world, and simply watch the living shells moving peacefully in a world free of talk, but one that God has made and that is a story too.

Both *Murexes*—*Murex brandaris* and *Murex trunculus* (my father, an oceanographer as well as officer, had taught me to learn their scientific names and respect those names)--had spines, but *brandaris* had longer ones, as if more afraid of the world. Why one would have longer spines than the other, even though they both traveled the same sand at the same time of day and ate the same things and had the same enemies—or why *trunculus* was banded like a tiger and *brandaris* was a solid pale yellow, I had no idea, but wondering about such things was what life was about, wasn't it?

When I was out of the water, I didn't bother drying off. I was sitting on my towel looking at my French book, *Les Conchilles de la Mediterranee*, my hands still a little wet, when I heard feet behind me in the sand, a heavy breathing, and I turned, startled.

It was the girl the older boy had wakened near sea's edge and she was staring at me--not smiling, not frowning—just staring. She was wearing the same dress, and she was pretty—a little strange with her triangular face and little mouth, but still pretty, like a picture from an old book. A girl from another time, an engraving—a girl someone had once loved long ago. Her pitch black hair was a mess—unwashed—but somehow this didn't make her less beautiful. It made her more like the cove, the beach, the seaweed drying in the sun—how could that not be pretty?

She was gangly, big-boned, her skin like porcelain; and I thought of a delicate, blind fish I'd once seen in a tide pool at another sea. She had a chipped front tooth, and her dress—whose flowers seemed huge to me now and very orange—looked as unwashed as her salty, sticky hair. She was standing alarmingly close, and I looked up at her with the friendliest face I could make.

She was still panting, as if she'd been running—though I saw no one else on the beach who could have been chasing her—and she was close enough that I could smell her breath, garlic and something else--something pleasant. It wasn't strange, her breath. It was the breath of a girl who'd perhaps eaten a late lunch of what the villagers in Vecchia Lerici ate, nothing more.

I was wet from swimming. I had my T-shirt on, and my wet shorts; and I was feeling very self-conscious. I had a book and had been teased for that before at the beach. I held the book tightly in my lap, as if, spine-like, it might protect me.

She laughed, leaned down, and grabbed at the book. I pulled it away, frowning. "What are you doing?" I said in Italian, annoyed. She was laughing, and I didn't want to be laughed at.

She got down on her knees, very close, and poked first at my bare knee, then my arm, still laughing. She said a word--it was a question--but I didn't recognize it. You can tell someone not to grab your book, but how to tell a stranger to stop poking you without sounding like an idiot? I had no idea, so I said simply, "Stop!"

"Stop!" she mimicked, and sat down beside me.

Was she "slow" or "simple," as the villagers put it? You could be without looking any different from anyone else. The boy on the beach that day had been a relative or a family friend; and if she were simple or slow, he knew she needed watching over. Was that why he'd been at the beach with his girlfriend and had gone down to water's edge to wake her?

This explained some things, but not everything; and I wasn't thinking very clearly at the moment. The girl had sat down beside me now, way too close. Our knees were touching. She was pretty, and my body felt like someone had set fire to it.

She sat up straight, made a funny, priggish expression as if to say, "I will now be proper," and said, "*Sono Livia, una ragazza.*"

I am Livia, a girl.

It was a funny thing to say, and I almost laughed. But we were touching, and she was saying, "What do you call yourself?"

"I am called Brahd-lee."

"Brahd-lee?"

"Yes."

"*Va bene.*" *Very well.*

There was something odd about her accent, I remember thinking, but again, how could I possibly think clearly enough even to think it?

She pointed at the book again. "*Mostramelo.*"

I'd never heard the expression before, but it was certainly Italian, and it obviously meant, "Show me."

Was this a dialect from the provinces? Was she from another region — far north or south? Her words also sounded archaic, like the Italian we'd memorized from the prologue to *The Iliad*. *Cantami, o diva, del pelide Achille, l'ira funesta....* But that was silly. I just didn't know enough dialects.

She was too interesting and pretty in her strange way — like a new kind of seashell, or a dream, or a new story — not to want her to stay. I was less terrified now — I'd survived her touch — and I couldn't stop looking at the fine, dark hair on her arms and legs. I opened the book and showed her.

"Seashells," I said. *Conchiglie.*

"*Ma il libro è scritto in francese,*" I added. *The book is written in French.*

She laughed again, and then, amazingly enough, uttered a string of French words. I couldn't follow them, but they were rhythmic, like poetry, and I thought I heard rhymes; so I nodded, as if I understood, and smiled, looking at her face again—her eyes, the dark hair that covered her forehead, her tiny mouth.

I jerked. She was touching my arm with one finger, her head cocked, as if fascinated by my freckles. Her own skin was perfectly white, no marks. The hair on my own arms and legs was yellow, but what interested her most was the freckles. She looked concerned, but it was play-concern. She poked at a freckle. I jerked again; and then she was speaking another line— rhythmic and pretty—but in Italian, Italian that felt old:

"Come i brillianti capelli sollevati da sua testa!"
Like the bright hair lifted from his head!

Her touch drove me crazy. She was full of life, wild, and so, even if she was simple or slow, I was hypnotized. If she wanted to poke me, that was okay. Why wouldn't it be?

I showed her the page with the two Roman-dye *Murexes* on it; and, as I did, she leaned in against me to see them, her shoulder against mine, her breath on my neck. My heart was beating like a tiny circus. The fire in me had no intention of stopping. And my arm, where she'd touched it, was itching like crazy.

"Si!" she said to let me know that she understood. But I went ahead, because I wanted to, and told her, my eyes on the book instead of her, in my best if halting Italian, about the *Murexes*-- how they lived in all the coves, how the Romans had used them, how the fishermen's nets caught them, how many specimens of them I had myself, how I collected seashells and always had, and, and, and…..

When I ran out of words, I stared at the book and waited. Her weight was against me. She was breathing hard and I wasn't breathing at all.

"They are," she said suddenly in Italian, "your heart's desire!"

This did not sound like a "simple" or "slow" girl. I turned to look at her face and she was grinning.

Maybe crazy then, I told myself. *Not slow, just crazy.*

"Yes," I heard myself say. "My heart's desire."

"And they--these treasures of the sea--return your love, do they not?"

What an amazing thing for someone to say, I remember thinking. The words were hers now, not poetry she was reciting, and they were words she was giving to *me*.

I had a little stack of seashells beside me, ones I'd collected from water's edge before swimming, and I gave her the nicest *Murex brandaris* from it—one that had died recently, been cleaned by the tiny crustaceans that do their work in coves, and one with three spines longer and more curved than they should be. A special specimen, and I wanted her to have it.

She was saying "*Grazie, ragazzo mio*" —"Thank you, boy of mine," and all I could do was blink.

And then the boy was there, his feet kicking sand up and into us as he arrived running, panting.

"Livia! You know better than that."

"I know better than the waves," she answered, sitting up, but leaving her hand on my arm. "I know better than the storms," she said, looking at me instead, smiling. It sounded like poetry again, what she was saying, the rhythm and rhymes in Italian, but it also sounded like her words—a poetry she made simply by talking.

"*Questo ragazzo è Brahd-lee*," she said, looking back at him again. *This boy is Brahd-lee.*

"You can't come down here alone, Livia."

The boy had barely glanced at me. I was not important to the situation.

"Do I appear to you to be alone?" she answered.

"You know what I mean. If you come down here alone again, you will not be allowed to leave the apartment for a week. Uncle will make it so."

"Unless I wish to."

"Even if you wish to. You know what Zio has said. Why do you this? You make me worry. You make us all worry."

She was getting up, sighing, but getting up, as if she knew she'd have to leave no matter how many words—or how much

125

poetry — were spoken.

"Go!" the boy said to her, and she started walking up the sand toward Vecchia Lerici and its dark alleys. She turned to look at me once — which made me happy — and held the *Murex* high, so that I could see it, then made a mischievous face as if to say, "Let's do it again!"

Which of course made the boy shout, "Go! Or I will tell both *Zio* and *Zia* that you have been bad."

As she walked on toward the alleys, the boy, who towered over me and would've even if I hadn't still been sitting in the sand, looked down at me at last, sighed too, and said:

"You are the American boy from the middle school. Your father is a Naval officer who works in La Spezia."

"*Si.*" He knew from my red hair, of course.

"You are a good boy, people say."

"I hope so," I answered, knowing it sounded stupid.

"She enjoyed being with you. That was clear."

I wished he'd said, "She obviously likes you," but he was being practical. He was worried about her. Nothing else mattered.

"That means she will do it again if she can."

"Do what?" I asked quietly.

"Come to find you."

I was sure he was going to add, "So please do not come here again." I held my breath and waited.

Instead he said, "If she does this again, there is something you must know."

I waited. I had no idea what he was going to say now. "She is crazy." "You must not treat her badly." "You must bring her home. Our apartment number is…."

"She has a disorder," he said.

"Excuse me?"

"She has a nerve disorder. It is one that makes her fall asleep at certain moments, and for no reason, though sometimes it occurs when she laughs. It is called *narcolessia*. If you are ever with her — if she has disobeyed my father and found you here —

126

please do not let her swim. It is the only fear we really have. If she swims and has an attack, she will drown."

I was staring at him, mouth open, when he added: "But if she falls asleep on the beach, that is fine. She will wake when she wakes...."

I took a breath at last. This was her cousin, not her brother, and she'd had one of her attacks the day I first saw her. She'd fallen asleep near water's edge, and he'd worried about her, and so he'd woken her. He'd been here with his girlfriend to watch over her—just as I'd thought--and they'd taken her to the beach because she loved the beach. She'd fallen asleep and he'd woken her. It was that simple.

I was feeling like family at that moment. To be included in her life. At the same time I was feeling, as her cousin wanted me to, *responsible*. He had no problem with me being with her—I was a "good boy," the village said—but in exchange I'd need to protect her. If she started to swim when I was with her, I'd have to stop her.

I waited him to say, "She's also crazy," but he didn't, and I was happy he didn't. How could I kiss her—something I'd already imagined doing--if she were crazy? That would be taking advantage of her. It would be wrong.

I sighed in relief and nodded.

"*Va bene*," he said.

I wanted to ask why she spoke the way she did—when his own Italian was like my friends'--but I knew that wasn't the point of this conversation. The point of it was her disorder, which we'd now discussed and had our understanding over, and so were done. He was a boy who was nearly a man—from a family in Old Town, a working class family—and men like that were practical.

As he walked toward Vecchia Lerici, too, I scanned for Livia in the windows of the apartments, but of course didn't see her. I couldn't stop thinking about her skin, my own freckles, the *Murex* I'd given her, and I was scratching my arm where she'd touched it because it was itching like crazy again.

The itching would get worse, and to say that I didn't know that would be a lie. She'd touch me again, I knew, because we both would want her to.

But the rash and the rest wouldn't start until later.

I rushed back to the cove the next day after school, and there she was. Her cousin was with her, sitting high on the sand fifty or sixty feet away, listening to a portable radio, his girlfriend not with him this time.

Livia was definitely waiting for me. I'd brought a paper bag with some of my best shells—ones I had duplicates of—and the same book (I didn't want to take chances)—and an even larger towel, so we'd both have room to lie down if she wanted to. I felt sly and excited, but anxious. I'd never done such a thing with a girl.

That she didn't have a towel of her own—I could see that from where I stood--was wonderful. Now she'd *have* to sit on mine.

She'd been making a design in the sand—I could see that—and she looked beautiful sitting cross-legged in the same dress by it. But what I really wanted to see was her funny tooth, her dirty hair, her white arms, and hear her laugh.

When I reached her, she said, "*Ciao*, Brahd-lee!" and grinned and wiggled just a little and laughed her laugh.

I stood there for a moment, looking at her cousin. He looked back, and then, to my relief, waved. It was okay, he was telling me. It was okay that I'd come to see her.

She was going to direct things this time, I could tell. I spread my big towel out, but she stayed where she was, picked up a seashell—a bright orange scallop--from the pile of seashells by her, and waited for me to pay attention. When I looked her in the eye, she placed the scallop on the sand, and this completed the design. It was as if I were the scallop—my hair just as orange--and she'd been waiting for me to arrive to finish it. She put me—the scallop, I mean—in the outer circle of the design. That circle was made of scallops and turban snails, alternating, and all the same size. Inside that circle was another circle, one made of the banded *Murex* and of pink cone shells, all pointing clockwise; and inside that circle, another, this one of tiny brown conchs and white Venus clams pointing counter-clockwise; and inside that, yet another circle, one made of *Thais* shells, tiny Mediterranean abalone and the largest *Turitella* shells I'd seen in these coves, all pointing clockwise, too. Inside that final circle, she had placed a little collection of spiny cockles, their matching halves placed in the sand so that they looked like hearts. There were hundreds of shells in the circles. How long had it taken her to make it?

"*Che bel disegno*," I said. *What a pretty design.*

"*Grazie!*" she said, waiting. What she was waiting for I had no idea. She had closed her eyes and her lips were moving, but I couldn't hear anything. And then I did. They were words I couldn't make out, but they were words; and there was rhythm and, unless I was imagining it, rhyme too. And it was not just how quietly she was speaking that made it hard to understand her; it was how the sentences were constructed and the strangeness of some of the words.

I was next to her on my towel, the circles of shells in front of us. I was looking at her, not at the design—I could have looked at her all day--when something jumped in the corner of my eye. I looked down at the design, but it didn't happen again. Something had moved, hadn't it? Had she tossed a shell or sand into the circle? Had her foot, which was almost touching the outer circle, moved, and that's what I'd seen?

Maybe my eye had simply twitched from looking at her so hard. Eyes could do that.

She was looking back at her cousin now. She looked sneaky, as if she were about to do something he would disapprove of and would stop if he saw it.

Then she looked at me and didn't look away. It wasn't a conspiratorial look. It was suddenly peaceful.

Please God – make her love me, I was thinking.

Something moved again in the corner of my eye--on the

sand, in the circle--but I couldn't take my eyes off her face; and, besides, her eyes seemed to be saying, "Yes, look at me — don't look *there*."

Something moved a third time, and I looked at the design.

"*No!*" she said, but too late. Three of the shells in the circle had indeed moved, turning, and I caught the end of their turns. I blinked. Were they still alive--did they still have living animals in them? It was three snails that had moved.

I reached out to pick one up — one of the *Turitellas* that had moved — but she caught my hand, laughing. She was shaking her head, a mocking reprimand, and when I tried to touch the shell again, she held onto me. Her hand was cold, but warmed quickly and felt wonderful. I let our hands drop to my knee and there they stayed.

"*Dopo*," she said. *Later*.

She was looking back at her cousin again, and so was I. We were both being sneaky now. Could he see that she was holding my hand? A good boy wouldn't be holding her hand.

I looked at our hands on my knee and remembered to breathe.

She made a little sound, and I looked up to see her eyes widen. She was still looking at her cousin, who was, I saw, getting up now and, without looking at us, starting to walk toward Vecchia Lerici. He hadn't picked up his towel and radio, but he was leaving.

I was excited because she was excited — I could feel it in her hand--I could hear it in her breath, which was quick and sharp. Were we going to kiss? Was that what all of this was about? Did she always kiss a new boy (I wasn't the first boy she'd played with on the beach — he'd as much as said that) when her cousin was out of sight?

I didn't know what to think. I wasn't even sure what I wanted.

Instead of leaning over and kissing me or squeezing my hand or poking at the freckles on my arm with a finger, she pulled her hand free of mine and said, "*Adesso*."

Now.

Before I could feel the disappointment, she was reciting another poem — one with words like *selvaggio* and *Vento* and *respiro* — *wild* and *wind* and *breath*--and, even though I was sure it was a dream — that I was suddenly sick or asleep or very crazy--the seashells in the circles began to dance a few inches above the sand.

Each shell is a word, a voice whispered, and I don't know to this day whether it was the village speaking, or the girl, or the man who had written that poem long ago, and not in Italian at all. It was, I like to think, all three of them, for that would be a greater truth.

As she spoke each word, a shell rose, danced in the air, and remained until all of the shells from the circle were there, dancing in the air, and they were the poem.

She was saying — and I could understand it because she wished me to:

"*Ognuno come cadavere, fino a quando*" —
Each like a corpse within its grave, until —
"*La tua azzurra sorella della Primavera suonerà*" —
Thine azure sister of the Spring shall blow —

Why I wasn't a little afraid of what was happening, I don't know, unless it was because she didn't wish me to be.

I reached out, unable not to, to touch one of the dancing shells, but she took my hand gently and stopped it again, shaking her head, but smiling, too. I didn't mind. I wanted to be touching her more than I wanted to touch any shell.

Then, staring at the dancing shells — the poem finished as words, but still there in the air before us — she brought my hand to her lips and kissed it. She wasn't looking at me. She was looking at the shells, and there were tears in her eyes.

I had no idea what to do. What kind of kiss was this?

I surprised myself. I pulled my hand away from hers and put my arm around her; and we sat for a while that way, she tipped against me, the shells dancing, both of us watching them. I glanced once or twice at her face, at the tears, but simply held her against me because that seemed right.

And then, suddenly, the seashells fell to the sand and we both turned, and I pulled my arm from her.

Her cousin was standing behind us. He had returned with a bag of food and was looking down at us. I assumed he'd be angry--that we were touching, that I had my arm around her, but he wasn't. He said, "Here is some food, if you would like it," put the bag beside us, and walked back to his place high on the sand. What he'd seen was an American boy, one the village spoke well of, with his arm around a girl who had tears in her eyes and was consoling her in her sadness.

Whether he had seen the dancing shells, I didn't know, but he probably had, and it didn't matter.

When he was gone, and we were eating a pear with some cheese, I happened to look at my arm and saw the rash. The itching had continued since she'd first touched my freckles, and I'd been scratching the itch even when I was asleep. My parents had noticed it, the scratch marks, but I'd told them nothing. Maybe a bush in the olive groves? I'd offered. There hadn't been any rash yesterday, only freckles and scratch marks. Had I scratched it raw?

No, it was a rash. Greenish and bluish, with an angry red around its edges, and a scaliness. I'd heard of psoriasis — everyone had--but this wasn't like the pictures I'd seen.

I started to scratch at it, but Livia's hand beat me to it. She touched the spot, let her fingers remain, and for a moment the itch left.

"*Mi manchi, Papà,*" I heard her say, and looked at her eyes. *I miss you, Father.*

I had never seen such sadness--even in my father's eyes when his mother died, or my mother's when she thought of babies.

She left her hand on my arm, her fingers on the rash, and I was happy to sit there with her. We sat for a long time looking out at the sea, at each other, at the shells that lay motionless now in the sand, saying nothing. And when her cousin finally stood up to walk over to us again, my self-consciousness was gone. We had sat for a long time.

"*Dobbiamo partire, Livia,*" her cousin announced suddenly behind us. *We have to go, Livia.*

"*Si,*" she answered, getting up. To me she said simply, "*Ciao,*" and I said the same, and so did her cousin, and that was the end of the second day.

That night, with her hand no longer on my arm to soothe it, the itching began again, ferociously, and by morning it had spread.

I tried to swim at the cove the next day, thinking the salt water might help it. I wore long pants and a T-shirt out of a new self-consciousness—I had the rash on my legs too--but still swam, waiting for Livia to appear. But the salt water hurt the rash. The spots were even redder and rougher when I came out, and stayed that way. Even the sand—the salt in the sand--hurt, so I was sitting on my big towel when she finally arrived. I wasn't going to swim again, especially in front of her, since she couldn't.

She was alone. She smiled, but did not sit down. Instead, she went to a spot in the sand—one that had no pattern as far as I could see—dug a few inches down, and removed a piece of cloth that held the shells she'd collected. Then, sitting on the edge of my towel, where she could reach the sand, she began to make another design—this one a six-sided star--and when she was through, she recited another poem until the shells began to dance again. It was real. There was no doubt.

Tears filled her eyes once more, but, again, she made no sound. She just watched the shells dancing, stared past them to a place only she knew, while her cousin—whom I hadn't noticed at first—watched us from his place high on the sand, as if he knew what story this was, what story was being told, and there was nothing to be done about it.

When it was time for her to go, I helped her bury her shells again, the ones she used over and over; held her hand for a moment that could never be long enough; and, though I wanted to follow her home this time, stand at her apartment's stairs in an alley and talk like people in movies did, I let her go without a word.

The rash got worse, and with it came dreams. The first night I was a body floating in the sea, tiny creatures filling my eyes, nibbling at my skin--because I was dead and the sea takes back what dies in its embrace. The second, a body--white as the belly of a fish—flailing, then drowning; and then, though dead, held by arms until I could breathe and wake, only to drown again, breathe and drown. And the third, a scaly body, green, flailing too, trying to breathe, to leave the sea…to *live* and scamper. They repeated and married, these dreams, and in all of them I became something I was not, but would if I remained here too long; and I'd wake from them itching, scratching, shaking, and wanting—like a baby or dying man or tiny lizard--someone to hold me.

I didn't tell my parents about the dreams, but they finally heard me making sounds at night—shouts and cries and moans--and knew something needed to be done. But at first it was just the rash. I couldn't keep it from them. I'd started wearing long pants, and even a long-sleeve shirt to dinner, but that just made them suspicious. Within a few days they were giving me the third degree and I had to show them my arms and legs. My mother was horrified and made an appointment for me to see the doctors in Livorno.

Because they heard from someone in the village that I'd been playing with a girl--a stange girl from Vecchia Lerici—and at a cove I didn't usually go to, one on the shadow side of the castle--and that I'd been there more than once, and secretively--my parents thought I'd caught my rash either from her or from the cove. Vecchia Lerici, the old part of town, *looked* dirty—as if it might harbor diseases the rest of the village wouldn't—and that was enough. Like so many adults, my parents trusted until they stopped trusting; and a friend of theirs from the NATO Center had, after all, gotten food poisoning at a restaurant in Vecchia Lerici.

They asked me about the girl--whether she had the rash too. I'm sure I turned red. Why not ask whether we had made out, or worse?

"I haven't seen her in a bathing suit," I said, wanting to let them know I couldn't have done much with her if she was fully clothed. "She's got a disorder--*narcosomething*--and she's not allowed to swim because she might fall asleep in the water and drown. So she doesn't wear a bathing suit."

My mother and father looked at each other, as if my monologue had told them exactly what I hadn't wanted to: How much I liked her. "A lie that's a little too long to be true," as my dad used to say.

"We didn't ask that. We asked whether she had a rash."

"None that I could see," I said. I didn't add that she did have a few tiny scars on her arms and legs, and one beauty mark (I'd never have called it a "mole") on her left leg. I didn't add that if she'd had even a pinhead-sized spot of the rash on any visible part of her body I'd have known it.

"Maybe something you thought was a scrape," my dad asked, reading my mind.

"No," I said quietly.

In Livorno that Friday I had to tell my story--as much as I was willing to tell about Livia--to the doctors. I was obviously not, in their eyes, "sexually active," and, experienced as they were, they could detect hypochondria (which ran, along with *verminophobia*—a fear of germs—in my mother's family) a million miles away. They did want to find out what the rash was, but they also knew they'd have to humor the wife of a Navy officer. *Was it serious?* she'd ask. *Probably not*, they'd answer. *It's not shingles. It's not psoriasis. Rashes are common with kids; and when it comes to symptoms, if it can be a zebra or a horse, it's probably a horse.* Angry at even the hint that she might be a hypochondriac, she would persist: *Is it impetigo?* (*No.*) *Is it psoriasis?* (*As I said…..*) *Is it an allergy?* (*Probably. We'll test him.*).

She had her own medical symptoms book, of course—they knew the type--and so would keep the list going for more than one session.

"It isn't impetigo, psoriasis or any of the other more common possibilities," they told my parents at the second appointment, after I'd had the tests. "It may be a food allergy we haven't yet identified or an 'environmental sensitivity' of some kind—so something at home or where he spends a lot of time, like--

"Like the water?" my mother interrupted.

"The water?"

"The water at the cove where he's been spending a lot of time."

This was embarrassing—and not just to me. You could see my dad was feeling it too, for me, but he stayed quiet. It would need—this conversation—to take its course, or there would be hell to pay when we were home. Hypochondria could not be denied its due, I knew.

"Have other children or adults gotten the same rash?" the doctor asked.

"No...." she conceded.

"Does sewage empty into that cove?"

My dad couldn't stand it any longer. "Other than a little street run-off," he interjected, "no...."

She glared at him.

"Then I doubt it's the cove water. The water along this coast is very clean."

"Then what about the girl?"

We'd been through this before, and you could see the doctor's eyes wanting to roll back.

"Does she have the rash?"

"Not according to our son."

The doctor was embarrassed for me, too. I could tell. I was fifteen, and it was a girl we were talking about; and this wasn't mononucleosis, after all. I looked at him, and he smiled: *I'm sorry.*

"Then I doubt it. I mentioned the possibility last time only as a remote one, and one contingent on her having it."

"So what do we do about it?" my mother asked.

"Wait to see if it gets worse, and in the meantime try to see if exposure to anything--not just food ingested, but anything else--paints, cleaning solvents, other household chemicals--seem to make it worse. It isn't bacterial or viral, and that would be the major concern. It also is not a symptom of any organ damage or dysfunction. The blood work would have shown that."

For weeks my parents took notes on everything—food, dish soap, car oil--that might be producing the rash. Since I was prohibited from going to the cove—from seeing Livia—the rash didn't get worse, but it didn't get better; and the dreams were just as bad. I was going crazy not seeing her, and she was in my dreams now, too, drowning with me, our dead bodies—blue from the cold, our skin leaving us—floating beside me, or mine alone, lying on the sand, and she making circles of seashells around me until I gasped, sat up and breathed once more; or both of us, small and green and quick, flying across the sand like laughter. But at least the rash wasn't spreading.

The next time I saw her, I felt like a criminal. If someone saw us together and word got back to my parents, I'd just lie, I told myself, and say it wasn't me. I didn't care if they didn't believe me. I had to see her.

This time, as we sat in the sand, I was barely aware of the salt's burning. She was staring at the patches on my hands and arms--really looking at them for the first time--and had turned serious, as if she understood what they meant even if I didn't. Finally she said, "These are you, my boy, and yet they are not. Do you want them to go away?"

"No," I answered, because I was afraid it meant I couldn't see her again.

I helped her collect new shells, watched her make a new design, and once more sat with her while she recited its poem and the seashells danced in a dream that was as real as the sand

and lapping waves and my beating heart. The one time I looked up at her cousin, he was asleep on his towel. His girlfriend wasn't with him this day either.

When it was time for me to leave, Livia held my hand and stared into my eyes, as if seeing me for the first time, and for the first time I was able to look back without nervousness or fear — for the opposite of fear, I knew even then somehow, was love.

I returned the next day; and, though it would be the last time I would ever see her, I didn't know that and it didn't feel that way. I was happy. I could sneak away like this every day to see her — I could do it forever--and everything would be okay, wouldn't it? Even if my rash covered my body and I looked like a monster, and I screamed all night, everything would be okay.

She was standing at water's edge, looking like she was a listening to something--or someone--and like she might walk into the little waves. This made me nervous; and when I saw her cousin wasn't in his usual spot, the nervousness got worse. What if she'd gone swimming and no one had been there?

I frowned. She turned, caught me frowning, and laughed.

Sometimes it happens when she laughs, he'd said.

Do people laugh when they swim alone? I didn't know.

There was only one pattern in the sand — between her and me--and it, too, was near water's edge. Had she made it hours ago, when the tide was farther out, or had she put it there on purpose, so the water would take it?

When I walked toward the pattern, she did too, and when we both reached it she said:

"*Stava scrivendo questo poco prima di morire.*"

I didn't want to understand her — I tried not to--but I did.

This is what he was writing when he died.

I looked at the shells, but they didn't move this time; they didn't rise in the air.

"*Il trionfo della vita,*" she said.

The triumph of life.

The poet had died, but this was a triumph of life?

138

She saw the question.

"*E il titolo che scelse….*"

That is the title he chose….

I looked at the shells again, and, again none of them moved. Again, she knew my question.

"*Non concluse l'opera….*"

He didn't finish it.

For this reason the shells wouldn't dance?

I started to ask, but she was saying:

"*Oggi succede.*"   *Today it happens.*

"*Che succederà oggi?*" I answered. *What happens today?*

"*Vado con lui.*"

Three simple words — and the worst she could have spoken.

I go with him.

"*Dove?*" I asked. *Where?*

The question did not interest her. She was removing her clothes. I stared dumbfounded. I looked frantically up and down the beach, at the sand where her cousin usually sat, at Vecchia Lerici, at the castle, hoping that no one could see, but also hoping that someone would come running.

"No!" I said. She was taking her clothes off, and that meant only one thing — that was she going to swim. I was responsible. Her cousin had made me responsible.

"No!" I shouted again, but she was out of her dress, out of her underwear, and I was *not* going to grab her, touch her; and if I was looking at her — at a nakedness I'd daydreamed about so many times--it was through horror.

To make it worse, she was walking toward the waves and over her shoulder saying:

"*Vieni con me, ragazzo.*"

Come with me, boy.

"You can't do this! Your disorder!"

She laughed, of course, and the laughter became a chill running down my back like a white-hot wire.

She was in the water now, up to her thighs, and I was right behind her. I'd failed to keep her clothes on her — I'd failed to do that--but I was not going to let her swim even if I had to touch her.

I grabbed her arm. She let me, but it didn't stop her. I held on and she dragged me with her. Within moments we were to our chests, the sand under our feet, a seashell here, a seashell there, touching our toes, the red-dye *Murexes* and others.

"*Nuota con me, così potrò annegare.*"

My brain froze. Whatever story this was, I didn't want to be a part of it.

Swim with me so that I may drown.

"No...."

"*Nuota con me, per favore.*"

Swim with me, please. Dance with me forever...in the sea.

I had no choice. If I didn't swim, she might indeed drown; and if I swam with her, she wouldn't.

She began swimming across the cove, and I followed, muscles burning in fatigue, the rash feeling like acid. My clothes pulled at me, weighing me down, and I wondered suddenly -- the terrible joke of it--if I would drown first.

Do not make her laugh, a voice echoed.

Crazy as she was, she might laugh on her own; and if she did, and had an attack, I'd need to be where I could see her face, to know it. I'd have to grab her instantly, hold her head up, and pull her to shore, burning muscles or no burning muscles --

And if my muscles cramped?

Yes, even then, even if I drowned doing it, becoming the body I dreamed of being every night.

I stayed with her, dog-paddling and breast-stroking and dog-paddling more, making sure I could see her expression -- nothing was more important than that--and all of a sudden she was looking at me with a sleepy smile. I panicked again.

But she wasn't having an attack. She was just tired. She wanted to look at me because, I saw then, my face made her happy, and smile at me, and tell me she wanted to go in, which she did.

"*Sono stanca, Brahd-lee.*"

I am tired.

She didn't need my help, and I was again too shy to touch her; but when she stepped from the water, I couldn't look away. Her hair was a soggy mess, her skin blue from the cold, and, though it was a body I'd dreamed of and loved, for a moment it wasn't hers at all. It belonged to another, and long ago.

She didn't mind at all that I was looking at her. She didn't hurry to put on her clothes. Instead, she looked out at the sea, southward, toward Viareggio, and then, as she glanced back at me, at my own soggy clothes and matted hair and relieved expression, she laughed. She hadn't laughed the entire time we'd been swimming, but she laughed now, and it was different, full of affection but also something else.

"*Sei meraviglioso,*" she said to me, and then added: "*E ti ho amato come lei ha amato lui – per un momento cosi breve.*"

You are wonderful, and I have loved you as she loved him – for the briefest moment.

My heart jumped and my breath stopped--not because of the words, which spoke of love, but because of what I heard beyond them:

That this story was ending.

Then, still laughing, she collapsed on the sand by her clothes, and for a moment was indeed a body drowned. And because the story, I knew, was not yet finished — and because I'd been wanting to for so long, and imagined she'd wanted it as well--I knelt down to make sure she was breathing (she was), pushed her hair from her face to see her eyes (which were closed), turned her face toward me, and, without caring who might be watching from afar, kissed her on the lips--and somehow did not die.

She stirred, eyes still closed, but stayed asleep. Had she smiled a little? I prayed she had.

I put my towel over her to block the breeze and cover her nakedness; folded her clothes and put them under her head; and, not knowing what else to do, waited until her cousin appeared at last, which he did, running.

He was angry, of course — his eyes flashed with it when he reached us--but not at me. He wasn't angry with her either. He was angry at the world, at a village, what it made of human lives by its magic, and forever. *This was going to happen and we could not stop it — we never can stop it*, his eyes were saying as he looked down at me and didn't say a word.

He was able to wake her by sitting her up and shaking her shoulders. When she was awake, he said something to her, then joined me where I stood, so that our backs were to her as she dressed. He still didn't say anything, and neither did I, and only when we heard her say "*Basta*" did we turn around to look at her, wet and sandy but at least dressed again.

When he took her away, she still looked sleepy--still in the sea drowning and happy — and when she looked at me, she couldn't see me. I knew that even then.

My rash had bloomed and the dreams had only gotten worse, leaving me exhausted and shaking, even if I hid the shaking well. But somehow, though I covered my cries at night with pillows, in the way that people know things without knowing how, my parents knew what I'd done — that I'd indeed gone back to the cove to see her. They told me I had to come home after school each day, that I had to stay in the house on the weekends. I disobeyed, of course. I went back the next day and Livia wasn't there. I was a little late getting home, but not enough to get screamed at. I went back four days in a row, staying at the cove for hours the fourth day; and it was at the wharf, on my way back from the cove that day, feeling as unhappy as I'd ever felt, that I heard what had happened from the last person I would have imagined I would.

The man without a throat, who spent his days at the wharf, was a widower, had lost his throat to cancer years before, wore a red bandana to cover the hole, and indeed spoke by spitting air. As if waiting for me that day, he waved me over, just as he often did when I was there to fish alone or with friends. We

142

hadn't talked in weeks, and I liked him, and he knew this. Some people were impatient with his spitting, with how hard it was to understand his "words of air" sometimes; but I'd never found it hard, and we'd talked many times, about many things.

He made the words slowly, but made them he did:

"She is his last descendant."

"What?"

"That girl is his last descendant here."

"Whose?"

"The poet's. The one who drowned."

I stared, not understanding, and then, with a sudden clarity — one that I knew came because the village wished it--I remembered what the villagers had been saying for two years, and the two stories I'd heard, separate before, became one.

A famous poet....

A strange young woman on the beach, walking as she often walked the coves where she helped bless the fishing nets and, like others of her kind, always would.

Finding the poet on the sand, wet in his ragged clothes, not breathing, his skin white as the moon, and rough where creatures of the sea had begun to nibble it away.

Recognizing him because she'd seen him often in the village, on his new boat or with his good friend, another Englishman, or with his wife in their evening passeggiata on the piazza.

Kneeling down beside him, then lifting him, cold and lifeless as he was, to hold him in her arms while, with a single kiss and a design of seashells on the sand, she used the only spell she knew that could bring to life something from the sea.

And he, the poet, waking for the briefest moment, opening his eyes, saw her and loved her because life loves what gives it life; and before her spell could fade and the sea could take him back, she removed her own clothes, took him inside her, and made a child of his that would live when others had not.

The family had taken her away (the man without a throat was saying to me now, his red bandana bright in the sun) because she had almost drowned.

I answered, "She didn't 'nearly drown'--I was with her, *Signore*," and he said, "You are a boy, so it doesn't matter. She *could* have drowned, *ragazzo*."

"But she knew…"

"Knew what?

"*The story.*"

The man was looking at me like I was crazy, or I knew too much. But it didn't matter. She was gone. Her family had taken her away.

"Where is she?"

"They are still traveling. She will be in a government hospital in Rome. They want her to be safe, not to drown because she thinks too much about a poet. She should be blessing the nets, of course, though that she will never do."

"But she is….a witch."

He looked at me again.

"Some say, because it is a legend in Liguria, that she is the daughter of the devil, one of seven, but you and I both know this is not true. She is special, yes, but she is still a girl—only that."

"She will be so far from the sea," I said weakly.

"And that is how it should be."

"*She needs to be near the sea.*"

"Not if she is to live—which you too must want, yes?"

"Of course."

How did he know these things?

He saw the question in my eyes.

"Her uncle is my cousin, and the boy you have met is my godson. This is how it is here. They have asked me to tell you."

He could also have said, *The village knows, and so we all know*, but he did not. He could have said, *This is the story too.*

She would, I knew, sit in her room in that hospital and (if she had a window), look out at the gardens (if the hospital had them), and in her mind's eye, remembering lives that were not hers, return to the sea each day…and swim there until she found him, and God took her too.

But will she think of me? I wondered, because love, like magic, can be selfish.

X

CANTICLE OF THE ANIMALS

I did not go to the cove. I did not go near the sea for weeks. After school, I avoided my friends and walked the olive groves around our house, spending hours with the bright green lizards. They got used to me and stopped looking up as if to say, "Do you not have better things to do?" Yet the rash re-appeared, this time worse — a scaliness that itched so badly I wanted to scream. Despite a dozen trips to Livorno, and ointments and anti-histamines and more silly changes in my diet, the doctors were at a total loss and finally had no more suggestions.

My parents decided one day that it was Lerici itself — not one thing, but many things — that was making me sick, and that it wasn't good for me to be there all the time. That I was starting to have even worse nightmares — ones involving bleeding children, ghosts, drownings, and scaly creatures of all sizes — didn't help. That I would start crying for no reason didn't help either. They were worried, and all they knew was that it had started — the rash and nightmares and the weepiness — in our third year of being there.

The first place they took me — to get away from the village-- was Carrara, the great marble quarry of the Etruscans, Romans and Michelangelo, and to the caverns of blue water inside the mountain there. I sat in the car staring at the marble dust that, like a dry, warm snow, covered everything, even the cars that had been parked there too long. I was barely aware that we weren't in Lerici. I saw lizards on the marble blocks, even though the lizards weren't really there; and when my farther suggested that there weren't any, not any that he could see, I got angry, argued with him, then fell silent again in a sadness not unlike my mother's. I heard a baby crying in the car next to us, but there was no baby. I felt water in my lungs, though the nearest sea was kilometers away. I missed Livia, but could have never have found the strength to follow her, even if I'd known

147

how, to Rome and her hospital, or even to crawl to the beach at the Magra River not far away and drown for her.

I wanted only to crawl onto a marble block in the sun, lie there warm and peaceful in the light; but I was too big, my arms and legs and hands and feet big as a giant's, and the wrong shapes; and, besides, people wouldn't have let me lie on a rock.

The next place they took me was the "City of Flowers," where we stayed in a *pensione* overlooking the Ponte Vecchio and the Arno River, and went to museums—because they would not disturb me. My legs worked under me, taking me from room to room, onto buses with my parents and off again, and finally back to our rooms; but I was no more present there than I had been in Carrara. After a week of Florence, my parents seemed as sad as I was. I'd done that to them. They weren't scratching rashes--they weren't hallucinating lizards on museum walls, as I was, or hearing Livia's voice or the nurse's in the old hospital or a crying child--but they were just as sad. They weren't *changing*, as I was—as I knew I was--but they were doing their best, by sadness, to join me, to keep me company, in a place I could not find the strength to leave.

The morning that our reservations at the *pensione* ended, my mother, who was not a religious person, said:

"Assisi! We need to go to Assisi, Charles. It's beautiful. Didn't the Paulsons go there last year? It has to have animals— St. Francis' animals--exactly what Brad loves."

Her words did nothing to me. They were just words, and I could hear behind them the slithering of something, a scampering, the whisper of scales, the lapping of water on an empty beach, a body lying somewhere to my right, motionless, and the faint footsteps of someone I cared about moving away from me in the sand.

Leave we did--because my parents did not know what else to do--even if my father, who was no more religious than my mother, wasn't sure why we were heading to Assisi. People thought it was gorgeous. Was that it? At least it was close. Just past the ancient university city of Perugia with its bright fashions, to the southeast, in the marble hills of Umbria. It would take us only a few hours.

We'd been taught all about it in our religion class. Father Tamillo, a priest who loved his little motorcycle and good food, also loved Assisi. He'd visited it many times. It was the birthplace of a saint, a man who in his humility and devotion had spent a life (and risked it) praising the beauty and innocence of the world's lowly creatures, whether they were sparrows or snakes or rabbits or the poor and powerless among us. It was the place where, to show that all human beings were equal in God's eyes, he had preached not from a pulpit high above his congregation, but standing on the dirt below them. The place where, later in life, he had found a grotto in a hill overlooking the city, prayed there with his brothers, and, in the end, passed his last hours.

There was a sacred forest, a *bosca sacra*, there, too — one of the two he had frequented in Umbria on his way to becoming a saint — though the thought of it filled me with a strange fear. *The trees are older than time*, a voice said, and a scaly tail twitched behind my eyes.

The city of Assisi was beautiful, but above it was a shadowy forest of twisted oaks and ancient stones walls covered with green lizards. Father Tamillo had said this, too, because I'd asked him. I'd asked about lizards.

Francis and Clare. *Chiara*. That had been her name. The girl. Father Tamillo had explained it until we were bored. She'd loved the young man named Francis, and had come to love God through him. She had started her own order, the Order of Clares, who were Franciscan women. Wasn't that how Father Tamillo had put it?

Francis had known Clare when he'd prayed here. They had known each other since she was 19. Father Tamillo loved this story, too, and who could not? A Romeo and Juliet that ended not with poison, but with an earthly love exchanged for something better. Who could not love Clare for loving Francis, and Francis for loving her, and both of them for loving something beyond this world--enough to give up their bodies without the slightest complaint?

The car hit a bump, and I understood: We weren't going to Assisi to pray, to ask God to heal me (my parents never prayed — they just didn't). *No. We were going there so my dad could take pictures! For his collection of cities!*

Exhausted from thinking — thinking that led everywhere and nowhere — I fell asleep in the car. As I did, my mother said, "He's falling asleep, Charles — thank God"; and I remember thinking *They are thinking about God. Maybe they do want to pray!* I could feel the entire world grow calm. My arms felt little and skinny and strange, my skin even stranger, but I could feel the world turn happy...and peaceful.

We stayed in the oak forest at an unpretentious villa that had been turned into a hotel. The estate had once housed cattle and horses, and their stalls were now a big, open-air restaurant. The first day I sat staring at the hummingbirds that came to the dozens of feeders that hung from the canopy over the restaurant tables, watched the sparrows fight over crumbs of bread, and held still while the green lizards darted here and there from sunlight to shadow, looking at me for no more than an instant as they went about their business. They weren't like the lizards of the witch whose husband had been poisoned — at least I didn't think they were — but they were still the lizards of this country, brave, playful, like children in Peter Pan suits, and it was nice to sit at a table watching them and the sparrows and the hummingbirds and daydream.

But after three days of this, my father, worried but trying not to show it, said, "We should do something--have an adventure."

"Yes, an adventure," I said, waiting.

"We should," my mother said, serious, perhaps a little embarrassed by the idea, "go to the grotto where Saint Francis prayed. Most tourists don't know about it. They just stay in town and go to the cathedrals. Don't you think we should go to the grotto where Saint Francis prayed with the other Franciscans?"

"Yes, I do, Susan," my father said. They had rehearsed it and were not great actors. But why not go? There would be birds and lizards there too, wouldn't there?

The hotel was on the road to the grotto, but whether to walk or take our car, we had no idea. My father asked the waiter. "It is a steep grade," the man answered. He was looking at me, and I'm sure I appeared weak—like the kind of "sensitive" kid who in the old days would have contracted consumption and died young. The kind of young man who studied too hard, who, though he loved Nature, was always pale, and who, for the sake of Intellect or Art, was willing to die at a romantically young age.

The man could also see the rash on my hands.

"You should take your car," he added.

At the top of hill we parked in a little dirt parking lot where a proud lot-keeper helped us maneuver our car to the spot he thought it should be and waved away any tip. Then we walked through the shadows of the oak forest, the sacred forest, on the dirt and leaf path that led up and up to the grotto, which nature, my father explained to us—or someone did—or someone already had, so I somehow already knew it--had formed millions of years ago in a marble fissure, in the same pink and white marble the city of Assisi was made from.

There were lizards here and there on the wall that ran alongside the dirt path. They sunned themselves in patches of light; but it was when we reached the archway and the gate that led into the little monastery that had been built centuries ago around the grotto, maintained by quiet Franciscans, that I knew at last why we were here. It was as my mother had put it--she had put it that way, hadn't she? *This is the place where a saint loved animals. Like you, Brad. You love the creatures of this country — even those in your dreams that do not exist — and that is why we are here. We have brought you to see them. The man who loved the animals did not weep in sadness. He knew only light. Doesn't this make sense now, Brad?*

Whether it was really my mother's voice or someone else's, I didn't know, but it made sense. The archway, lit by bright sunlight, was *covered* with lizards.

I couldn't even blink. I just stared at them, grinning.

The monk that greeted us there saw me look at them and smiled. My father saw the smile, and looked too, and saw them. My mother was talking and did not. There were hundreds of lizards on the archway, like a wreath, which was impossible — the green wall lizards of Italy did not swarm — they never swarmed--but there they were. And why not? Why shouldn't they swarm? Why wouldn't creatures want to be at a sacred place like this, a peaceful monastery where no one wished anyone ill, with enough bugs and sun for any lizard who chose, like a tiny pilgrim or penitent, to come…and never leave?

The monk hadn't thought these things consciously any more than my parents had, but he understood them, I knew. I could see it in his eyes, which glittered like jewels in the sun.

I stared at the lizards, not wanting to leave them. My father had my elbow, but I didn't take a step. The monk was unhurried. It did not bother him to wait while a boy looked at lizards that should not have been there but were.

The lizards stared back. And then, though I never imagined they would, they said:

You are here because of what is about to happen, they said; and the voice, like my mother's a moment ago, was in my head, but also not.

You are here so that you might remember what you imagine you have forgotten, so that you might become what you have always been.

My father pulled at my elbow, laughing a little as he did when he was nervous. I moved, stepping through the gate at last, looking back once at the blanket of little green bodies covering the archway. They were following me with their heads and eyes, and the monk, I knew, was watching it all.

"What do you keep looking at, Brad?" my mother asked.

"The lizards…."

"Well, there are *definitely* lizards there," she said, relieved. "They're all over the place, aren't they, Charles?"

"Yes, they certainly are."

I followed my parents to the grotto itself. There was little to see. What it had been like when St. Francis first found it and prayed there, alone and with his fellow monks, no one really knew. Coolness, darkness, peace. Over the centuries since his death (or so my mother recited from her guidebook), his followers had "improved" the grotto. They had built steps down to the grotto, then enclosed the stairway in stone, then added rooms with stone, then bricked some of the rooms shut, then made other little rooms with altars and shafts of light entering them, then added more brick and mortar and stone, until the grotto was but a tiny little room with a satin chord keeping you from kneeling where Francis had knelt. It wasn't a grotto any more. It was a room made by human beings in the belief that he was more loved by God than they could ever be.

My father took pictures because my mother wanted him to, but also because he loved to. She would say, "Take a picture of Brad here. Take a picture of Brad over there, too." He would obey, happy.

"Take a picture of Brad in front of that prayer room," she was saying now, and it was indeed a beautiful little room.

"Try to get that bluish light," she added.

As he positioned me in front of the little wrought-iron door that kept people out of the prayer room — kept them from praying as Francis had prayed — I saw the lizard. I blinked. It was still there, and it should not have been. It was on the wall just behind my father. Lizards didn't come down into the earth like this, where it was cold and damp and there was no light. This one was here. To remind me —

153

Of what?

That the story isn't over.

"He's doing it again," my mother said quietly. "He's staring."

"It's just a lizard, Mom. I *like* lizards."

"I know that," she said, "but do you have to stare like that — like you're a million miles away?"

"It's fine," my dad said bravely. She glared at him.

"No, it isn't."

"Well," he said gently, "we're not going to fix it down here, are we?"

That was a funny thing to say, so I laughed. My mother glared.

"The lizard likes you, too," I heard myself say, and for once my mother was speechless. She was looking at the lizard, too. She had no words.

Flash! went the camera, and that was that. The lizard was gone, and my mother was fussing again, bossy, worried.

When we were in the courtyard again, I could hear a few voices drifting from parts of the monastery, but not many. Three or four different languages, spoken softly, a laugh, a respectful silence, more silences than sounds, but even the silence had a calm music to it: The whisper of a breeze, the cooing of pigeons or doves, the beating of a heart in your ears.

"Shall we go top-deck?" my father asked.

"Sure, Dad."

As we climbed the stairs from the courtyard to the patio high above it, I noticed the pigeon resting under the eaves. I hadn't seen it before because it had been so still. Whether it had been the source of the cooing, I didn't know. It was the only pigeon I'd seen there, and it was white as the whitest dove.

I smiled. It was a part of the story being told, but what part did it play?

The bird was bigger and fatter than a dove, but it was pure white — I'd never seen a pigeon so white--and it did look like a dove, and, if that's all you had to tell the story, that was good

154

enough, wasn't it?

I laughed. My mother turned, stared at me, then looked back up the steps.

From the patio we looked down at the great valley below Assisi, as still as an old painting, but with the first start of a haze that would in time become the smog I knew from the States. The olive trees and little oaks couldn't defeat it. They would try, do their best, breathing in and out and in and out, but it would not be enough, and the autos and factories in the valley would win eventually. But that was all right. These were things of the body, of the earth, and did not really matter.

When we returned to the monastery's gate, the priest was still there with his smile. My father asked where the sacred forest was.

"It is around us," the priest answered.

It always is, the voice said.

"Ah, yes," my father said. He never got frustrated with people. He was a born "executive officer." He could make peace anywhere. He could mediate anything. The Navy knew what it had.

"Can we walk through the forest?" my father asked.

"Yes, of course, *Signore.* The path starts at the other end of the courtyard."

So we took it. Because I lagged so much these days when I went anywhere with my parents, they walked ahead of me. Had they walked beside me, we would never have moved.

The path wound along the side of a forested hill, where you could turn and look back at the monastery, its pink and white face staring at you, a steep creek running by it to the forest below.

In a moment, the path had rounded the hill and, since my parents were ahead of me—my mother chattering about something that made her happy—I was alone and stopped.

Looking down the hillside through the little oaks, I wondered what made a sacred forest *sacred.*

Little birds twitted here and there, and something larger—a rabbit maybe—ran through the leaves of the forest floor. The sun reached down through the trees and made a painting of light on those leaves. The rabbit did not want me to see him, so I did not. But the rabbit was there, just as I was.

But was this any holier than any other forest?

What would Francis say?

I looked down at my feet, and there were seven—I counted them slowly to make sure—seven lizards –seven lizards looking up at me. Lizards did not live in families; they did not travel in groups like this. This was part of the story, too--to help me understand.

The lizards waited.

"Ah," I said, sounding like my father.

Yes! one of the lizards said. *Ah!*

They were, I saw, indeed the same kind of lizard loved by the witch of the olive groves at home.

Come, one of the lizards said.

And so, down the hillside—away from the path and through the trees--we went.

I listened for my father's voice, calling, but did not hear it. If my parents couldn't find me, they'd think I'd returned to the monastery. Perhaps I could beat them back. I didn't want them to worry, but what was there here for them to worry about?

The lizards moved together at my feet, leading, and I had no trouble seeing them because they were green against the brown oak leaves, and the green glowed as if each had a piece of sunlight burning under his skin. They were little lights, and I followed them.

At the bottom of the hill, near the creek that started above the monastery and here widened into a gushy stream, I stopped and looked down. The lizards were gone. This made no sense.

How can it be over?

A sound—a footstep in the leaves across the creek—made me look up.

On the hillside across from me was a figure. It was watching me.

It was not a man. It was bigger than man, and shaped wrongly.

It was an animal.

It was a "man-deer," as the children of Lerici called them. A cervo. A stag. These forests had had them once, but not for a long time — and not one so old and big. It couldn't be here, yet it was.

Its antlers stretched like the limbs of a tree.

The creature looked at me, and I looked back, and in a flapping of wings another creature joined it, steadying itself on the antlers. The stag didn't flinch, didn't toss its head.

The owl — nearly white — turned its head this way and that and finally stopped, staring at me, too.

It was impossible, this scene, but it was the story that needed to be told, the one I was helping to tell even though it was the village telling it.

I understood.

A stag and an owl. A man and a woman. Here forever....

Something rustled at my feet. I looked down. The lizards had returned, jumping up on my cuffs like puppies.

I laughed. "I know how to get home."

They wanted to lead me, so I let them, turning once to look back at the stag and its friend on the hillside. Neither had moved.

I know who you are, I told them.

Yes, they answered, *you do*.

The next morning my parents announced that they wanted to see St. Clare's cathedral, which was down in the city itself. They asked if I wanted to go with them.

I said I was sure the cathedral was beautiful — since it was *Santa Chiara*'s — but that I wanted to go back to the grotto.

My mother wanted to say, and with no little sarcasm, "To watch the lizards, I suppose," but she didn't. She didn't want to start the day off badly. She didn't want to be unkind.

"It's pretty there," I said. "It's peaceful. I'd like to walk around and then sit for a while."

I'd be safe there, they were thinking. And wasn't this why they'd brought me? To get me away from Lerici, where I could be at peace and my rash might improve and I wouldn't weep for no reason. Besides, the priests there would watch over me, and there were always a few tourists, too.

Without a word they decided.

"Well," my father said cheerfully, "stay on the paths, and don't sprain your ankle the way I did."

He'd gone skiing the year before—we all had—a week in Austria; and as his boss at the center had given him permission to go, he'd said to my father, "Just don't sprain your ankle." My father had sprained it.

It was a joke—the corny kind my dad loved.

"Yes," my mother chimed in, "stay on the path. Don't go down in the forest the way you did yesterday."

"Mom," I said. "It's a forest, not a jungle. I'll be fine. If I go into the forest, I won't go far."

I wasn't going to stay on the path, and she knew it. Why pretend?

"All right, but *stai sicuro*, Brad." She loved using the Italian she knew.

The lizards found me earlier than I'd expected. As I took the path from the grotto—the one that wound through the sacred forest--they appeared like a line of little watchdogs in front of me. *We can't allow you to pass!* they shouted. *You must obey us. Otherwise, you'll sprain your ankle.* They laughed hard, and so did I. *Besides, you know where we are taking you and you want to go, yes?*

Yes, I said, delighted.

They led me down the hill again; and again, there was the stag and the owl. The stag was drinking from the creek, and the owl had to steady itself as the stag's head dipped and rose and dipped again.

The owl looked at me, eyes wide in the daylight.

If you know who we are, the voice said, *you know why we are here.*

It is your forest, I answered. *It is yours forever.*

Yes....

The yellow eyes blinked, waiting.

Did you choose this? I asked.

Yes.

I would've chosen it too, I heard myself say.

You may still.

Before I could say I didn't understand, the voice said:

Do you dream of scales? Of the brightest sun?

Yes, I answered.

One that warms the stones of the world forever?

Yes.

Come closer then.

Why I should've been afraid, I didn't know, but I was. To be this close to them, to the bodies they had chosen seven hundred years ago....

I walked toward the creek. The closer I got, the bigger the stag looked. It stopped drinking at last, raising its head and gazing at me.

Can you not see what your rash is? the stag asked, or was it the owl, or both? Did it matter?

Sometimes I think I can.

It is your beginning, the stag said.

Come closer, the owl said again.

I took four steps, stopping in front of the stag. Had he turned his head, his antlers would have knocked me over. I could smell the scent of him now—the dank earthiness, the sweet musk.

Give me your arm, the stag said.

Shaking, I held my right arm out. As I did, the long sleeve—I always wore long sleeves to hide the rash—pulled back, and the scaly, iridescent skin showed itself.

He snorted and took a small step toward me.

The step brought his muzzle to my arm, and I felt his hot breath.

The rash began to burn, the scales shifted, growing clearer, the iridescence turning green —

The owl, balancing on the antlers, moved its wings, and a wingtip brushed my arm.

The green skin brightened.

The stag breathed again on my arm, and the green held, covering me. Everything around me grew huge in an instant. The nearby water of the creek was a tidal wave. The trees were the height of mountains. The stag's legs were like trees. The face of the owl was a great moon.

I looked to my right. There, someone like me--skin like green jewels, a long tail, twitchy feet—looked at me with big eyes. I moved toward him, and the motion took me skittering. I moved again, and the stag—or someone somewhere--laughed like thunder as creatures just like me scampered over, put their feet on my head, wrapped their tails in mine, welcoming me. *You're one of us!* they said, happy as children. *Stay with us forever!*

You did know, the stag was saying.

Of course, I heard myself answer.

My brothers and sisters, with their emerald skin, toes and tails, and cheerful twitter, formed a line. I joined them. Together we scampered down the side of the hill. Behind us the earth shook from the stag's hooves, the air thundered with the owl's wings. Where they were taking me, I didn't know. It didn't matter.

I barely remember what I did that afternoon, with them. I was what I could become if I wished it; and it is by the bodies we have in this life that we understand the world. I barely remember what it was like, except for the peace of it.

I certainly don't remember the walk home. I had a scratch or two on my legs and arms and face — as if animals had scrambled over me with their claws—but nothing else. My parents commented on my face. "A branch," I explained. They did not see the other marks.

My mother was excited. "Santa Chiara is the most beautiful

little cathedral I have ever seen."

It was good to see her happy.

Because I seemed to be at peace--no weeping since we'd arrived in Assisi--and because my rash seemed to be less angry, not as red around the scaliness--we returned to Lerici the very next day. We drove through the medieval city of Perugia, which was beautiful too, a kind of sleepy Florence, and this made us happy, too.

For two weeks in Lerici I did not have nightmares. I did not weep. When the dreams and tears started up again, and were even worse, I knew what needed to be done.

Even if I could lie with creatures I loved, in the sun, in a light that did not end, I did not want to leave. I wanted to be with the people I knew and the people I would meet in my life — in this body.

To do this I would have to leave Lerici. Its stories were not mine.

I was lucky. My parents, too, knew I needed to leave. They knew that the doctors and trips were never going to help. They knew--somewhere inside them, though they could not have expressed it--that it was indeed the magic of the village that was making me sick, making me change.

The night came when I woke in my bedroom to fire — every inch of my skin roaring as it tried to become what I both wanted and didn't want it to be. My pajamas were gone — I'd thrown them somewhere in the darkness--and the sheet burned, too. My parents had heard my cries. As they rushed in, turning on the light--before I could cover myself completely with the sheet-- they saw what no parents should have to see: Their child covered with the tiniest of scales, sparkling like green frost.

I struggled out of bed, holding the sheet to me.

"Turn off the light!" I shouted. My father obeyed. My mother had screamed once, and he did not want her to have to scream again. He did not want to scream himself at the sight of me.

I fought. I made myself *feel* my skin, my human skin. When I did, the scales skittered sideways, away from mind's eye, only to take another piece of skin somewhere else. I clenched every muscle in my body. I made my skin taut. I beat at myself with my hands, but this made the scales skitter, too--like water flowing away and back again.

If every inch of my skin became scales, it would be over. It would happen in a flash, as it had that moment in Assisi—when the stag breathed on me and the owl touched me and the world changed because I had, too. I'd come back that time, but wouldn't this time.

If I couldn't stop the scales, it would be over.

Where was I? It was my bedroom, but it was the sea, and I was floating, a poet dreaming of a child as he drowned, while a child on a beach somewhere recited the poet's poems and dreamed of drowning. But it was also a crack in the earth leading to a light that would keep me and my green brothers and sisters warm forever if I would only let it. *You know you wish this*, the village said, and it was right, and yet I could not be its green skittering thing.

I held in my soul's eye the faces of my friends—Maurizio, Marco, Gianluca, Carlo--and our teacher, and Livia, and Ciccio, and even Keith and his brother, and my mother and father, who were there in the darkness with me, not saying a word, scared.

The fire on my skin burned without a flame, and yet the green scales glowed in the darkness. I heard my father gasp. My mother started to cry, helpless and hopeless, but then said, "No!"--telling herself, I knew, that anger was better than sadness, that anger might save her son if she only knew what to do with it.

"Leave him alone!" she shouted suddenly.

My father stepped toward me, wanting to help, too.

"Don't touch me." I said it gently, a quiet scream. He stopped moving. I was standing there, the sheet no longer against me, struggling inside my skin to keep it.

Brothers and sisters of the sun, it isn't time, I was saying, and

162

their little faces chattered, pleaded, cajoled. *If not now, when?*
When I no longer need this body.

This they did not wish to hear. They ran up and down my legs and arms, touching every inch of me with talons and tongues. I was lost.

"It is his body," my father said then. It was a voice I'd never heard him use and one I'd never hear him use again.

It is his *body!* my mother said, too--without words.

The lizards wouldn't give up. They were flowing now in wave after wave from the olive groves through the open window, covering me--my face, my eyes, my naked body. They squirmed between my fingers, in my ears, up my nose, between my toes—touching every piece of me they could; and as they touched it, the fire grew.

The room was growing larger, and I knew what this meant. It was nearly done—complete—and I'd soon join them, leaving with them on tiny feet through my bedroom window, lost to this world and to myself.

It is my *body!* I heard myself shout.

The room stopped growing. The lizards fell still.

It is my body, I shouted again, and a great sigh rose from the little bodies in the darkness.

Three voices had said it now.

The truth.

That my body was mine to leave or keep.

When the fire had faded—for the time being anyway—I reached down in the dark for the sheet and covered myself again.

"You can turn on the light, Dad," I said.

When he did, I could tell from their looks that my own face, though it might be red and scaly, like the rash had been before, was not the skin of a reptile.

They wanted to hug me, but did not know whether they should.

"I'm okay," I said, and, the sheet still around me, let them, and didn't scream when they touched me. Their touch was a balm to the fading fire. They were my parents, and I was still a boy.

That very night, with a trans-Atlantic phone call routed through NATO, my father asked for an emergency transfer — citing his son's "physical and emotional condition." By the next morning the Navy had granted it. An officer's family was important. A request like this was not one the Navy could say no to.

I didn't sleep that night. I couldn't. If I slept, it would happen again. My parents seemed to understand this, and they stayed awake with me, taking turns. They did the same the next night. The following morning we were on a flight to D.C., where my father had been assigned to the Navy's Department of Undersea Research. Professional movers hired by the Navy would clear out our house in Lerici, pack everything up and get the most essential things to us by military air in a few days. In the meantime, we'd stay in a hotel in Fairfax, the D.C. suburbs, where my father would commute to the Pentagon.

I slept on the plane because — well, because I was tired, but also because Lerici was a thousand miles away now; and, though I slept, the scales did not return. The lizards could not crawl over me. I woke to fire on my skin now and then, but that was all.

Our first night in the hotel I slept, too, waking from nightmares to my mother's or father's face, to their looks of concern as they inspected my skin, but found no glowing green. The rash was red, that was all. The nightmares were about a baby crying in the night where dead animals hung from trees, a hospital where a woman waited to heal a boy she loved but had never met, and a body floating in the sea while another woman dreamed her dream about a monster made by men, but not rooms growing larger as I grew small.

Within a week the rash was gone. My parents slept like babies while I walked the lobby and the streets of suburban

Virginia, happy to be back in the States, but also sad — about something I did not quite understand. My eyes teared up now and then from the sadness, but also from relief.

I started school mid-year. That same month my new doctor looked at me astonished when I told him about a rash that had only months before covered my entire body. "There is no evidence of that," he said, with a tone that said I was lying. He did not use that tone again, and I knew my parents had said something to him, or copies of my charts had reached him from Livorno, or both.

My parents looked at me oddly now and then — as if they didn't know me, as if they wanted me to tell them what had happened that night in my bedroom in Lerici hadn't really happened, or to explain it if indeed it had. Were they afraid? Of course. Were they afraid of *me*? A little, I think. But the fear faded. I was their son once more, my face their son's face, my voice his voice.

Within six months the lizards seemed but a dream. My Italian faded quickly, as if I wanted it to. I remembered my friends in Lerici, of course, but they were far away — like people in someone else's story. Even the thought of the village didn't make my heart race, though a part of me — a dangerous part — did miss it. That was the sadness:

A path not taken.

A peace no body like this one will ever know.

In only four months I had a girlfriend named Emily — blonde hair, green eyes, a great smile--one who liked the Beach Boys, kissing at the movies or in my father's car, and sailing on Chesapeake Bay.

POSTSCRIPT

It took me thirty years to return. I wanted to see Lerici again before I died, but was afraid to go back. I'd married late in life. I'd become a teacher and had had children of my own at last. When I returned to the village, it was to find those I'd cared about—those who knew the stories--and I found some, but not others.

The man without a throat, our hunchback teacher, and Livia, the girl at the beach—all had been taken by time. *A relapse of cancer…. A problem in the lungs…. The wrong mixture of medication at the hospital…..* These were the rumors, and not the only ones.

My best friends from school were middle-aged now, too, with jobs like architect and attorney and professor, and their own families. When I spoke of "magic," they laughed, teasing. "The American boy--*come romantico—come semplice! How romantic--how simple-minded!* They did remember what had happened to us, those stories, but they did not want to talk about them. "Magic?" they said, suddenly serious. "You must outgrow it, Brad. To live in this life you must."

The lizards on the walls of the brick paths and olive groves looked at me, but were just lizards. I couldn't hear their voices. The witches in the groves were dead because old women always die. The German hospital had burnt to the ground from a meaningless arson. The strange village of Magusa, with its crimson doorways, had been removed for a new road to Pisa.

When I took the hands of my son and daughters--whose love keeps me in this world and always will--and we stepped in our street clothes into the sea at the cove where fishing nets had once been dyed, nothing happened. No one called my name. No shells danced above the sand like a poem sung by a pretty girl or the long-dead poet who had written it. My skin did not burn. No rash appeared the next day, or the one after that.

The village had moved on, I saw--to other boys and other stories, as it would for eternity. But I--I couldn't let go. However long I lived, I'd keep writing about what had happened to me there, unable to resist it, never sure which stories were the *truest* --in the ways that matter most--or whether my body would ever really be my own.

For this is what its magic asked of me, and always would, as the village waited forever, singing to the only sea it would ever love.

XI

EPILOGUE

Sun and Stone

The American boy was a man of nearly eighty now, his children in distant cities, their children in other cities, too, his wife beating him to it (this thing called death), and his life had been full of more miracles than anyone deserved. He had six, maybe eight, months to live, according to his doctors, who fussed like terriers around him when he visited them on his own (which he was more than capable of doing); and that was fine – their fussing and the six or eight months – but he had not told his children yet. There were places he wanted to visit-- some new, but others from when he was a boy, living with his parents in a strange village on the Mediterranean Sea – and he needed to visit them alone. He suspected his children would forgive him. He had raised them to believe in something beyond what eyes could see and fingers touch, hadn't he? And, though they knew he loved them, he'd written each a reminder, one in which he'd also explained, as best he could, why he needed to travel alone.

The letters had been mailed two weeks ago in Rome, at the start of his travels. His children had certainly received them by now.

One of the places he needed to visit – the last one on his list, in fact- -was the pretty city of Assisi, which he had visited with his parents when he was so sick. Here he was again, on the sunniest of days, looking down on its pink and white marble face from the hill where its famous saint had prayed until the day he, too, had left this world.

This is where it would happen, he knew. He had known it for quite some time, but you can't rush life.

He remembered this--this monastery, its grotto--and yet in certain ways he did not. It was a mystery – the kind mystics spoke of-- something you could see and yet never really see. It had been a mystery then, too, when he was young, calling to him like one of Ulysses' sirens, even though both the grotto and the village on the sea that had sent him to it had made him ill, asking of him something he could not yet give.

The grotto (he did remember this), was simply a fracture in the marble of the hill, and could be reached only by the narrowing stairs of stone that turned and turned again. It had been walled in over time with brick and mortar so that there was only one room and an altar in it. It felt like a tomb, as perhaps it should, since the saint had died here, too.

He had toured the handful of rooms of the silent monastery – feeling a little nauseated (as the thing inside him often made him feel), but not weak, not breathless--and had peeked over a gate into the little chapel where the priests of this place met in prayer. Then he had returned to the entryway and the path that led from it to the parking lot, ready to leave. The Franciscan monk who had been there earlier was gone now, though the American thought he could hear him speaking to the middle-aged couple back in the courtyard.

When he stepped through the shadows of the entryway and into the sun, the lizards were still there on the wall, as he'd known they'd be, as if swarming, though this kind of lizard never swarmed. The sun was fading a little, but was still bright enough to hold them there on the stone. They looked like big-headed children in green tights, happy as children are when they are happy.

One of the lizards scampered toward him, stopping close enough that he could reach out and touch it, and stared at him, as if inviting him to step even closer. It was not a lizardly thing to do, but he was not surprised.

He had known there would be one.

"Thank you," the American said. "Thank you for coming."

He sat down on the wall by the lizard, which didn't move, and waited, watching the little creature. The thing looked back at him, its skin like the tiniest black and green fish eggs, or more accurately, like the exquisite, colorful "sand paper" made by one of his favorite artists, Tasaki, master paper-maker of Kyoto.

"Now?" the lizard asked suddenly, its voice scratchy, like a hinge needing oil, its jaw moving oddly so that it might make the words--the actual sounds of the words.

The American laughed so hard he could not answer. The lizard's eyes were like teardrops, he saw, but tears without sadness. What would they have to be sad about in a place like this?

Nothing at all, the lizard answered, hearing the man's question because in the oneness of things all questions, like their answers, could be heard. *Nothing at all,* the lizard repeated. *But is there reason for sadness anywhere?*

"Of course not," the American answered, aware that he was grinning like an idiot.

The lizard asked it again: "Now?"

The American laughed, but more quietly this time, as a peace – one he remembered from this place long ago--settled into him, along with a silly poem about a cat.

"Yes," he answered.

At that word, lizards began to come from the walls, from the drains in the cobbled pathway, and from the nearest tile roofs. The American held still as they covered him with their green bodies, tickling him with their toes, settling down at last on him to wait. He held still as his skin began to itch – as it had done so many years ago in that village by the sea – and to change, turning red, then purple, then green. It was difficult not to move as their bodies, hanging on him, seem to grow, bigger and heavier, but he knew this was only because his own was growing smaller. He closed his eyes, and in a moment none of it mattered.

The lizards parted, moving away, returning to their walls, drains and roofs. On the wall where the man had been, one lizard remained, its body still for a moment as it woke and blinked and moved in that jittery way all lizards move because something might, at any moment, grab them, and then where would they be?

As the sun fell and darkness began to fill the world, the lizards on the walls on either side of the entryway began to move. They did not enter the cracks and holes in the walls or find rotten pieces of oak wood on the sacred forest floor to hide under for the night. Instead, they gathered in twos and threes, then by the dozens, then hundreds, and made their way toward a hole in the easternmost wall, a hole no bigger than a man's hand, but one that wound down through the ancient stone upon which the monastery had been built and from which nature had long ago made the grotto itself, toward a light that burned in the earth, in a tiny cave no human had ever set foot in. The cave was oddly shaped, horizontal, no longer than a man and no wider, and there was no way that all of the lizards could fit into it even if they'd wanted to. Instead, they nestled against each other in the little tunnel and felt warm in the light of a sun that wasn't a sun, one that burned forever there.

The new lizard, though it had trailed behind the others at first, getting used to its legs, making sure they worked properly, had no trouble following. It knew where the others were going. It knew that light, but who didn't?

ABOUT THE AUTHOR

Bruce McAllister is best known for his science fiction, fantasy and literary fiction. His short stories have appeared in literary quarterlies, national magazines, themed anthologies, 'year's best' anthologies and college readers; won awards from *Glimmer Train* magazine and the National Endowment for the Arts; and been a finalist for the Hugo, Nebula and New Letters awards.

He is the author of two novels, *Humanity Prime* and *Dream Baby*, and the short story collection *The Girl Who Loved Animals and Other Stories*; and his articles on sports, popular science and writing craft have appeared in a variety of publications.

He lives in southern California with his wife, choreographer Amelie Hunter, and is now a full-time writer, writing coach and book and screenplay consultant.

www.mcallisterstories.com
www.mcallistercoaching.com

CPSIA information can be obtained
at www.ICGtesting.com
Printed in the USA
BVOW08s0730120717
489102BV00011B/175/P